Entwined Publishing books by L.M. Somerton

I0680906

The Retreat
Serving Him
Trusting Him
Finding Him

Fairground Attractions
Ghost Train
Merry-Go-Round
Helter Skelter

Treasure Trove Antiques
The Lucky Cat
The Gilded Mirror
The Poison Bottle
The Jeweled Egg

Anthologies
Racing Hearts: Keeping the Luck
His Rules: Tagging Mackenzie

Collections
Sold to the Billionaire: The Auction Lot
Family Business: Thunderclouds and Sunshine

THE 39 STEPS
A CONTEMPORARY REIMAGINING

L.M. SOMERTON

ENTWINED PUBLISHING

The 39 Steps: A Contemporary Reimagining
ISBN # 978-1-80250-244-2
©Copyright L.M. Somerton 2025
Cover Art by Kelly Martin ©Copyright May 2025
Interior text design by Entwined Publishing
Published by Evidence, an Entwined Publishing imprint

Published in 2025 by Entwined Publishing, United Kingdom.

Entwined Publishing is a division of Totally Entwined Group Limited.

THE 39 STEPS

A CONTEMPORARY REIMAGINING

Dedication

With thanks to John Buchan
for his inspiring work.

Preface

The 39 Steps is an adventure novel written in 1915 by Scottish author John Buchan. It was first published by William Blackwood and Sons, Edinburgh. It was serialized in *All-Story Weekly* issues of 5 and 12 June 1915, and in *Blackwood's Magazine* (credited to 'H. de V') between July and September 1915, before being published as a book in October that year. It is the first of five novels featuring Richard Hannay, an all-action hero with a stiff upper lip and a knack for getting himself out of tricky situations.

The book was dedicated to Buchan's friend Thomas Arthur Nelson. It was, as is often said nowadays, 'of its time' and much of the language and sentiment would not be appropriate today. This version follows a similar plot line but characters have been renamed and the point of view has switched from first to third person. There are some lines where I have adapted Buchan's beautiful descriptions of Scotland and if you are familiar with the original story (not the film adaptations—of which there are four—which are different) you'll spot similar elements to the plot in some places.

I've always loved Buchan's novel and hope I've done justice to the original with this modern version, which incorporates a romance — something that wasn't present in the 1915 book.

Chapter One

Oberon Wycherley left his City job as a management consultant about six o'clock one May afternoon, fed up and generally unimpressed with life, the universe and everything. After several years working abroad, he'd been back in the UK for six months, and it felt more like a century. He'd finally given in to the knee surgery he needed following a fall. Three months of recuperation had driven him part way round the bend then three months spent advising investors on mining companies' stocks around the globe had taken him the rest of the way. It did not make for a thrilling existence. Talking about mining didn't compare to being out there, on the ground, delving into actual holes in the earth.

He opted to walk home rather than face the hellscape that was the Tube in rush hour, and to give his knee some much needed exercise, but as he strolled along the road, it began to rain. The first gentle spattering soon turned into a persistent downpour.

"And of course today is the day I don't have an umbrella," he grumbled, turning up the collar of his jacket. "Perhaps weather forecasters would be more motivated to get it right if they were made to stand outside whenever they got it wrong." *In their underwear. Actually, that guy on breakfast TV is quite hot, I wouldn't mind exploring his meteorological preferences.* He was passing one of his favourite watering holes, Ye Olde Oak Tavern, and made a snap decision to stop in for a drink and wait out the deluge. He ducked into a narrow passage, which emerged into a courtyard boasting a cherry tree and a few scattered wooden barrels that served as tables in decent weather. *Chance would be a fine thing.* The Oak was one of those pubs that looked like it belonged to a forgotten age. It still sported a Victorian façade and had been there even longer than Victoria's reign. Since 1546 in fact, and if its walls had the ability to speak they'd probably be able to spill some very juicy Elizabethan gossip.

Brushing the water from his shoulders, Oberon pushed his way through the heavy oak door then paused to let his eyes adjust to the gloom. The interior space was divided into three small ground-floor rooms. Oberon went into the one housing the bar. Cups, beer mugs, and tankards dangled from the brown-lacquered ceiling. Bottles sat on a shelf at the top of the dark wooden panelling, which finished mid-way up the walls. Above them hung signs, drawings and Elizabethan memorabilia. Oberon liked the place because it was well hidden and attracted locals rather than tourists. Some of the old guys supping pints were as gnarled and stained as the ancient furniture.

He ran a hand through his soaked hair, grimacing at how wet he'd managed to get then went over to the bar. The barman, who would have made an excellent rugby prop forward, filled the small serving area completely. He spotted Oberon and grinned.

"Hey, blondie, running from the weather?"

"Evening, Marley, does it show?" Oberon took off his damp jacket. The water had soaked through to his shirt. Marley tossed him a bar towel.

"You look like a drowned rat. Try that."

After a bit of cursory drying, Oberon passed it back. He tuned into the background music. "Do you ever play anything but reggae in here?"

Marley shook out his dreads. "Why would I want to do that? My momma gave me this name for a reason, ya know."

"This isn't Bob Marley though, it's...Burning Spear."

"My influence is finally getting to you."

"I'll have a glass of something red. You pick." Oberon trusted his friend's judgement when it came to wine. Marley was a collector and quite a connoisseur.

"Try this." Marley poured him a large glass. "It's a nice medium-bodied malbec, from one of Argentina's oldest family-owned wineries."

Oberon sniffed the glass, swirled the ruby liquid around then took a sip. "Nice. Really smooth."

"Yeah, I bought in a few cases. I liked the fruity, spicy combo. Reminds me of me."

Taking a longer drink, Oberon savoured the taste. "It's excellent. Can you spare a couple of bottles?"

"Sure. I'm here to educate your palate as well as your ears. You look like you need cheering up. What's going on?"

"Oh, I don't know." Oberon settled onto a bar stool. "Depression. Malaise. General pissed-off-ness. I've been in the sun too long and this weather makes me miserable. My colleagues annoy me. I'm not getting enough exercise because of my stupid knee, and London's nightlife seems a bit flat."

"You're not looking in the right places, my man." Marley grinned.

"I'm a bit past quick hook-ups nowadays, Marley. The clubs are too loud. Fuck, I'm getting old, aren't I? Thirty something must be the new eighty something."

Marley's deep, rumbling laugh shook his frame. "Sounds like you're in a rut, Obi. You need some excitement to drag you outta there. Find yourself a cute twink who likes getting his ass spanked."

"Tempting. Very tempting. Talking of twinks, how is the Doc these days?" Marley's partner was a cute, bespectacled doctor who worshipped the ground Marley walked on.

"Good. Very good. Works too hard. Paediatrics can be tough, ya know?"

"I can imagine. Give him my best. Tell him I said to take a break and feed you grapes."

"That has interesting possibilities."

Oberon sipped his drink while Marley served other customers. The pub's clientele covered the entire spectrum of the population. It was known as gay-friendly but attracted young and old, purple-haired to pink-rinsed. Oberon enjoyed the laid-back vibe, which had everything to do with Marley's mellow personality.

"You look like you're miles away." Marley was back. "What's going on in that pretty head of yours? You back on a South African beach soaking up the rays?"

"I've been out of the country so long, I think I built a picture of what it was going to be like here and it isn't living up to expectations. I made decent money abroad, didn't have much to spend it on and planned to enjoy myself for a while. I thought I'd settle here, you know? Now, I'm not so sure."

"You left as a child, didn't you?"

"Haven't been back for more than brief visits since I was six," Oberon said. "My father was a diplomat and worked all over the world. I was home-schooled then went to Colorado School of Mines for my degree. I've worked in South America, Australia and all over Africa."

"And now you're back to wet weather, endless conversations about how wet the sodding weather *is* and tea. All the tea."

"Yeah. I'm done with sight-seeing, restaurants and theatres. I've caught up with odd remnants of family but they don't know me and they have their own lives. I'm thirty-five, I have a nice but temporary roof over my head, I'm in decent shape and I'm bored."

Marley poured another glass of wine. "Job not cutting it?"

"It pays the bills. I'm freelance for now, and consulting isn't the same as being out there getting my hands dirty. Sorry, I don't know why I'm so grumpy. I have it good compared to a lot of people. I shouldn't be whining at you."

"Part of the job, mate, listening to people moan." Marley took the sting out of his words with a chuckle.

"I'm gonna go sit in the corner and browse my phone like a normal human." Oberon paid for his drinks and the wine he'd be taking home with him then took his glass and snagged a table in the corner next to the window. His job meant keeping an eye on the news so he could justify a bit of doom-scrolling as work. The media sites were full of the usual rubbish about the royals, D-list celebrities and the cost of living. Oberon browsed anything he could find that was remotely related to mining and mining companies. There was a particularly interesting piece about deep seabed mining for polymetallic nodules. *Potato-sized lumps containing copper, cobalt, nickel and manganese…hmm, all crucial to battery manufacture.* The mention of potato was enough to make his stomach rumble. He took his glass back to the bar, said goodbye to Marley, who handed him a bag containing his bottles of wine, then headed for home.

The rain had stopped, leaving a fine, clear evening. Everything smelled freshly washed. As Oberon walked back to his flat near Portland Place, the crowds surged around him, busy and chattering, snapping pictures of anything and everything. He envied their easy-going camaraderie and excitement even if he didn't understand the attraction of countless selfies. The shop assistants, office workers in sharp suits, street cleaners and buskers all had things to do and places to be. He gave a few pound coins to a homeless guy hunched in a tatty sleeping bag in a closed-down shop doorway because he saw him yawn; he was a fellow-sufferer. At Oxford Circus, Oberon looked up at the sky and made a vow. *I'll give this place another week and if nothing exciting happens, I'll stick a pin in a map and buy a one-way flight.*

His short-term home was on the first floor of a newish block behind Langham Place. He was flat-sitting for a friend who'd taken a six-month engineering contract in Brazil and the rent he was charging Oberon was peanuts compared to the going rate in the area. The building was upmarket enough to merit a security desk in the entrance hall, along with mailboxes and a well-maintained noticeboard. The lobby smelled of lemons.

His friend had a cleaner who came in three times a week and though Oberon didn't make enough mess to justify it, he didn't want to take the woman's income.

Magdalena traded light duties for baking, leaving him Polish sweets and pastries that did nothing for his waistline. There was a lift, which Oberon rejected in favour of the stairs, thinking of those pastries.

He was fitting his key into the lock when another man made his way up the stairs. He moved quietly and his sudden appearance made Oberon start. He was slim, with a short reddish-brown beard, orange-streaked hair and washed-out grey eyes. He was half a head shorter than Oberon's six feet one.

"You're my upstairs neighbour, aren't you?" Oberon recognised him as the occupant of a flat on the next floor. They'd exchanged hellos once or twice in passing but nothing more.

"I am, Mr. Wycherley. I've been hanging around waiting for you," the man said. "Can I come in for a minute?" He seemed to be making an effort to steady his voice, and he reached for Oberon's arm but didn't touch him. "My name is Art Carew. I won't take up much of your time."

Oberon didn't feel he could refuse. He got his door open and motioned Art in. No sooner was Art over the threshold than he made a dash for the kitchen, where he peered out of the window before coming back.

"Is the door locked?" he asked, not waiting for a response before fastening the security chain in place himself. "I'm sorry," he said. "I'm taking advantage, but you look like the kind of man who might understand. I'm in trouble and I need a favour. It won't cost you anything."

Oberon debated throwing him out there and then but he was bored and the man was intriguing, if a bit odd. "I can't promise anything, but I'll listen. Can I get you a drink?" *He looks like he needs one.*

"That would be kind and very welcome."

There was a tray of decanters and glasses on a table next to the couch. Oberon poured his visitor a generous neat whisky. Art downed it in one. "Another?"

"Thank you but no. I should keep a clear head, but that one helped steady the nerves."

"My landlord appreciates a single malt. Take a seat. I'll just be a minute." Oberon carried his wine through to the kitchen then took off his jacket before returning to the living room. "So, tell me what's going on."

"Yeah, I should, shouldn't I?" Art said. "I'm a bit shaken up and not thinking straight. You see, I'm dead."

Barely repressing a snort of laughter, Oberon sat down in an armchair. "What does it feel like?" *Oh wow, this one's as nutty as a fruitcake.* His expression must have betrayed his thinking because Art cracked a smile.

"I haven't totally lost my marbles — yet. Listen, I've been keeping an eye on you, and you strike me as someone who can look after himself."

"You've been watching me?" *This is getting creepy.*

"Needs must. I swear I'm not some weird stalker. You don't seem the type to be easily scared and I'm in dire need of help."

"Can you get to the point?" Oberon said, becoming impatient. "I've had a long day. I haven't eaten yet and my patience is wearing a bit thin."

"Of course, sorry." Art squared his shoulders like he was gearing up for a big announcement. "As I said, my name is Carew, Art Carew. I'm American, as you can probably tell, from Kentucky. I inherited a bit of cash from a great uncle so after college, I decided to travel. I'd never been out of the States before. I majored in journalism, minored in modern languages, so I scored a freelance gig writing travel articles for a couple of papers and set up a travel blog. I spent two years in

Europe, moving around every few months, earning enough from writing to cover basic costs."

"Sounds like a good life. I've not spent that much time in Europe," Oberon said. "My work took me further afield."

"It was a good time, but I guess you don't need my entire life story. I'll cut it short. I got interested in environmental issues and that was the start of the dumpster fire my life has turned into."

Oberon settled back in his seat, prepared to give Art a hearing at least. "Okay, you've hooked me. Go on."

"I like to dig into stories. I dug a bit too far. You can probably guess the biggest environmental issues in Europe. Climate change, air and water pollution, biodiversity loss, waste management…the list goes on. I made friends with some people involved in ocean clean-up. It felt practical, you know, joining beach trash collections, snorkelling and scuba diving for plastics. Nothing radical."

"There's similar stuff going on here. Surfers Against Sewage is one organization."

"Yeah, well I started blogging about the clean-ups. I set up a YouTube channel and got divers to film what they were doing, that kind of thing. It gained some traction. People commented and asked questions. They were interested and the journalist in me wanted to investigate more."

Oberon poured Art another drink, this time well diluted with water. His hands shook when he took the glass but he sipped slowly. "I shouldn't, but thanks."

"Go on."

"Behind all the government rhetoric and empty promises, there's a shady movement out there, controlled by some very dangerous people. Not everyone wants to clean up or protect this lump of rock we all live on. They don't give a flying fuck for future generations, just money and power. These aren't thugs, they're educated, connected people. Some of them consider themselves saviours, conspiracy theorists that like to debunk science. But beside them are the investors playing for money. A clever man can make big profits on a falling market, and your average guy in the street doesn't understand how stocks and shares work. It happens in plain sight but if you know where to look…"

"So what is it you found out that's so important?"

Oberon listened as Art went into detailed background on companies and their alliances. People who had mysteriously disappeared or met with accidents. "The aim of the whole conspiracy is to discredit environmentalists, especially those with the loudest voices and deepest pockets."

"But why?" Oberon asked.

"A new world. An end to 'woke' liberalism. Debunk the environmentalists and climate change scientists, tell people how much more cash they'll have to pay for the basics when the cost of living is already so high and investment opportunities would open up for fossil fuel exploration, fracking, mining, habitat destruction…you name it. That's the goal. Huge money-making schemes and no conscience."

"That's not all, is it?"

"No and it's the reason I need to stay alive."

"But I thought you were dead."

"I'm coming to that. I guess you've heard of Kairos Doukas?"

That made Oberon start because he'd been reading about Doukas in The Oak earlier. "Greek multi-millionaire."

"Yeah. Doukas is a rare thing, an honest businessman. He's worth billions and he intends to start spending that money on some massive environmental concerns. He has the cash, and influence, to sway governments, Mr. Wycherley, and that's why he's got a target on his back." Art swallowed the remains of his whiskey. "Anyone could work that out, but I found out…how and when they intend to kill him. Knowledge that's potentially fatal, and that's why *I* had to die."

Oberon was still dubious but there were threads of interest in Art's story. *It's so outlandish, it might just be true.* "Who are *they* exactly?"

"The Black Stone. That's what they call themselves. So fucking pretentious. I'm surprised they didn't go for Spectre, but I guess it had already been taken. They're a small group of powerful people with similar interests and the money to get what they want."

"So…Doukas."

"They can't get to him in Greece, he's very well protected. Lives in a fortress. But on the fifteenth of June, he's coming here. The British government is hosting an international business schmooze-fest and he's the guest of honour. If things happen as planned, he'll never return to Athens."

"So get a warning to him. Make sure he stays at home. Pretty sure Greece in summer is a better option than London anyway."

"And play their game?" Art asked sharply. "If he doesn't come, they win. The opportunity to make his announcement on a world stage will be gone. It could be years before he's able to enact his plans if he has to deal with big businesses one by one. He'll never cut through the misinformation and noise these people will create. It's all about the timing."

"What about the British Government?" Oberon said. "They're not going to let their guests be murdered, it's not a good look. Even an anonymous tip would be taken seriously by the security services, I'd have thought."

"It might, and I've sent a letter to the head of MI5 on the slight chance they accept it's not from a crank. But, they could throw all the security in the world at the event and Doukas will still die. These people aren't playing games. They want a big stage just like he does. He'll be murdered unless I'm around to stop it."

"And how do you intend to do that?" *What can one man do, if this is all true?*

"I think I've told you enough for now. You'll want to check things out. If I were you, I'd be thinking I'm some weird American dude with a few screws loose. I'll tell you more when you've had a chance to do some digging of your own. Take care to cover your tracks though."

"At least tell me where you got the story from." *He's got me hooked.* Oberon couldn't help liking Art. The fire in his eyes could be fanaticism or it could be self-belief.

"From a friend who'd crewed on a certain industrialist's super yacht. A casual dinner conversation, would you believe? He was working as a steward to get passage from Cyprus to Monaco, which is where I ran into him. He was drunk when he told me what he'd overheard. That night he rode his moped off a cliff road. Or that's what it was made to look like."

"Jesus."

"It was then I decided it would be a good idea to disappear in case anyone checked into who he'd been with that night. People at the bar we were in could identify me easily enough."

"Sounds like a sensible move."

"I came here by a very roundabout route. I hitched from Monaco to Paris, changed my appearance and paid cash to take trains to Copenhagen. From there I caught a ferry to Norway and travelled to Bergen collecting stories for a travel blog — not too far from the truth. I flew to Scotland from Oslo then took a coach and two trains to get here."

"That must have thrown them off the scent."

"Until yesterday I thought I'd done a good job of covering my tracks. Then…I guess I fucked up somewhere. Electronic surveillance is difficult to avoid." He screwed his eyes shut, as if remembering distressed him.

"What happened?"

"I saw a man standing in the street outside this block a week ago. Big, bulky thug. I've been staying at my place all day, only going out after dark for a walk and supplies. I watched him for a bit from my window, and I thought I recognized him… He came in and must have spoken to the security guy — I found a business card in my mailbox. It was a warning."

There was naked fear in Art's eyes, convincing Oberon that he was telling what he believed to be the truth. "So what did you do next?" There was a new sharpness to Oberon's tone.

"Kill or be killed. Fight or flight. I'm done running, and I couldn't fight off a wet lettuce so there was only one way out. I had to die. If the people after me think I'm dead, they'll back off."

"How did you manage it?"

"In London you can get anything done if you have the cash. Influencers have made it easy with all the crazy-assed stunts they've pulled, so I created an imaginary one of my own. I hired an undertaker to turn up here with a van and a coffin, bought some stage make-up and watched enough YouTube videos to do a reasonable job at making myself look corpse-like on the remote chance anyone looked in the coffin. I seeded some stuff on my socials over the following days hinting that I wasn't well and would be taking a hiatus. My 'body' was taken away this morning and is currently in cold storage at the funeral home, where it will stay. If anyone investigates with them, they're tracking down my family overseas before the cremation. I made my way back here with the vague idea of finding you. I don't know many people here and none well enough to trust. We'd spoken a few times so you seemed as good a bet as any so I waited for you to come home because I couldn't go back to my place."

"How long did you spend in that coffin?" Oberon asked.

"Too long." Art shuddered. "I don't have a future as a vampire, that's for sure. It was a tad claustrophobic."

Oberon drummed a beat on his knee, thinking. "Rather you than me. Your story is almost crazy enough to be true."

"I can't prove any of it. These people are ruthless about covering their tracks."

"And it *isn't* some elaborate social media scam?"

Art shook his head. "I could have thought up something way better than this if I wanted to be an online star. Being dead isn't so much fun."

Oberon considered his options. "Right. I'll give you the benefit of the doubt and trust you're not yanking my chain. You can sleep in the spare room tonight. I'm going to order food because I'm starving. You want to clean up?" Looking closely, he could see traces of greyish make-up around Art's hairline. "My name's Oberon but you can call me Obi. Mr. Wycherley takes me back to public school and some uncomfortable encounters with a sadistic housemaster."

Some of the tension left Art's body. "I can't tell you how grateful I am. If you'd thrown me out on my ear, I don't know what I would have done. I'm pretty much out of options."

Oberon pointed Art at the bathroom then ordered Thai food, telling them to leave it at the desk. Half an hour later, Art emerged from the bathroom. The beard was no more, the red colour was gone from his hair leaving a dull brown and he had shaved a line through one eyebrow. He looked completely different and much younger.

"What do you think?" Every trace of an American accent had gone.

"Impressive! If I attempt an American accent, I end up landing somewhere between Irish and Australian."

"I'm now Theo Digby, a friend of yours from South Africa, staying with you on vacation. In case anyone notices there's someone else in your apartment and you need a cover story. I'll try to stay out of sight, though."

Oberon collected his Uber Eats delivery when it arrived. His guest ate like he was famished but was flagging and soon excused himself to bed. Oberon wasn't far behind him. He sat in bed feeling more animated than he had in months. *I might regret it, but I'm kind of glad something interesting is happening. Maybe that plane ticket can wait a while longer.*

The next morning, he awoke wondering if he'd imagined the events of the previous evening. Art, or Theo as he had named himself, showed up as toast popped out of the toaster.

"Hey, did you sleep well?"

"Against the odds, I did."

"I need to go to work as usual," Oberon said. "Will you be okay here? The fridge is stocked."

"You're amazing, Obi. I'll be fine. I won't be going anywhere."

"I've texted Magdalena, my cleaning lady, to give her the week off with pay. Told her I'm going away for a few days, so you shouldn't be disturbed. I'll finish work and get back here as early as I can."

"I appreciate you trusting me in your place."

"You're dead. What would you want to steal?"

Art stared at him then fell about laughing. "I needed that. My life has been far too serious recently. Thanks, Obi."

After leaving Art with the TV remote and instructions for the coffee maker, Oberon left. He spent a fidgety day at work, bought a pot of fresh soup and bread from an artisan deli on the way home and reached the flat around five.

The security guy was in the mood for a chat. "You weren't around yesterday when it happened, Mr. Wycherley. Your upstairs neighbour passed away. We had the undertakers here. Bad business."

"I think I passed him on the stairs a couple of times," Oberon said. "Didn't speak other than to say hello, you know how it is. What happened?"

"No idea. Undertakers didn't say who'd called them, but he was an American."

As if that explained everything. "Yeah? So new tenants soon?"

"He was paid up until the end of June, so there won't be any rush. Funeral guys need to track down his family. You might hear some noise when the packers come in, so thought I should let you know."

"I appreciate that." Oberon was amazed at the man's lack of curiosity. There were some big holes in Art's fictional death production that were obvious to him but maybe it was easier to take things at face value.

For the first two days Art stayed with Oberon, he was no trouble. He read, made a heap of jottings in a notebook, ate what Oberon gave him without complaint and slept for long hours.

Oberon did some of his own research, taking care to use incognito mode on the web. Everything he learned suggested that Art's story could be true but there was nothing to substantiate it. Underpinning Oberon's belief that his new flat mate was telling the truth was Art's obvious fear. Not being able to find concrete information was also telling to Oberon, as were some coincidences that couldn't be accidental.

That evening after dinner, Oberon brought up something he'd discovered.

"Did you know that The Black Stone is a rock set into the eastern corner of the Kaaba, the ancient building in the centre of the Grand Mosque in Mecca, Saudi Arabia? It's revered by Muslims as an Islamic relic which, according to Muslim tradition, dates back to the time of Adam and Eve."

"Who's an easy target to blame when a terrorist attack happens?" Art asked.

"Muslims."

"Yeah."

"Do these people want to start a war?"

"Imagine knowing what was coming, where to invest to make the most profits in the event of war, how valuable fossil fuels will become."

"They're leaving a fake trail."

"Indeed. This isn't a sudden thing, it's taken years of planning."

"Fuck."

"Yeah, that about sums up the situation."

By the third day, Art began to get restless. He commandeered a free calendar Oberon has been gifted by a local Chinese restaurant he frequented and ticked the days off with a red biro, making shorthand notes against them. He got edgy, starting at every noise and when Oberon returned from work, asked if he'd taken precautions not to be followed.

"It's not my own skin I'm worried for," Art said. "It's ensuring my plan succeeds. I'm going to tell you a bit more because if anything happens to me, I want there to be someone else who knows what's going on."

Oberon, watching the latest episode of a drama on Netflix, half-listened as Art talked.

"The threat to Kairos Doukas won't begin until he gets to London and it'll come from the highest echelons of society, the elite, people who would never be suspected. A woman, who uses the name Julia Kensington, is the key and will act as a decoy to get Doukas away from his security." Art talked about the Black Stone, a man with a lisp, and an old man with a young voice who could hood his eyes like a hawk.

To Oberon, it all seemed as melodramatic as the thriller he was watching but he let Art ramble.

The next day Art was much more cheerful, as if getting more of his story off his chest had relieved some hidden pressure. Oberon had a dinner date with a mining engineer he had to see about a possible consulting job and came home late at about half-past ten, mellowed by good wine and ready for bed. From the street he could see that the lights in his flat were not lit. *Odd, I guess Art's already in bed.* All was quiet as he made his way upstairs. Oberon snapped on the light switch but there was nobody there. Then he saw something in the far corner of the sitting room which made him stop dead. "Oh, fuck." His mellow mood dissipated instantly.

Art was lying on the floor, sprawled on his back. There was a long knife through his chest, which skewered him to the floor.

Chapter Two

"Well, that's me royally screwed." Oberon stared at the body and the blood seeping into cracks in the varnished floorboards. He was instantly ashamed that his first thought was a selfish one. Art was on his back, staring at the ceiling, eyes wide open. "He was being careful, paranoid, so what the hell happened?" It wouldn't have been difficult for a killer to get past the security desk. They would have waited for the guard to take a break and walked right past. "No cameras in the lobby either." Talking out loud helped. Oberon couldn't see if there were wounds on Art other than the obvious one and thanks to a lifetime of viewing thrillers, he knew better than to approach the body. He debated a stiff drink but he'd already had half a bottle of wine with dinner. "Need to keep a clear head. Think." He went to examine the front door to see if there was any sign of a forced entry, but there wasn't. "So he let his killer in himself. Why did he open the door?" Oberon checked the time. It was gone eleven.

He wasn't going to get any answers from Art and calling the police wasn't an option.

He searched the flat to make sure no one was hiding, which in retrospect he should have done sooner. "I'm not very good at this. Definitely wouldn't survive the next Scream movie." The killer was apparently long gone. Oberon closed all the curtains and put the chain on the door. Taking action, even something so mundane, helped clear his head and Oberon figured he had until the next morning to work out his next move. There was a possibility the killer might return but he didn't think that was likely.

I'm fucked. Well and truly fucked. Any doubt Oberon had about Art's story was gone. The proof was lying dead with a knife through his heart in the corner of the room. "Whoever was after you because of what you knew, caught up with you, didn't they, you poor sod?" *Why am I talking to a corpse?* Someone had made sure of Art's silence. Oberon's problem was that Art had been staying with him for four days. It would be safe to assume that Art's enemies would think he had told Oberon something to gain his trust and use of his spare room. "So that makes me next on the hit list." It might not happen straight away, but Oberon was certain his life was in danger. He gave serious consideration to calling the police but had no idea what he would say to them. "If I tell them the truth, they'll either laugh or I'll end up charged with murder. The circumstantial evidence is strong enough. Fuck." *Maybe that's the plan. Tie me up in the legal system long enough to kill Doukas regardless of what Art might have told me.* If he was arrested, Oberon had no close enough connections to put up bail money. *Not that bail would be offered, I'd be seen as a flight risk.* He'd be held on remand, unable to cause any trouble for Art Carew's mysterious enemies.

"If I played the odds and told the authorities what was going on...on the remote chance they'd believe me and not throw me in the psych ward, the bad guys would win. Doukas wouldn't travel, which according to Art is as good for them as killing him." Oberon paced, thinking through his options. Art's death coloured everything. Royston Wycherley had done his best to instil a sense of fair play in his son. Diplomacy often meant speaking up for the underdog and Oberon, like his dad, couldn't stand bullies. Art had stumbled on something bigger than he could deal with and he'd paid the ultimate price. Something deep in Oberon's psyche wouldn't allow him to let that go. He didn't consider himself to be either reckless or braver than anyone else, but at that moment, he was determined that Art's death wouldn't be meaningless. *I won't give up on him, Dad, Art deserves someone on his side.*

Oberon relocated to his bedroom so that he wouldn't have to keep looking at Art's lifeless body and staring eyes. He concocted several plans then rejected them all. Every path seemed to end with a gruesome death, something he'd rather avoid. After a stressful hour regretting several life choices, he came to the conclusion that he was going to have to follow Art's example and disappear. "And somehow stay under the radar until June fifteenth. Less than two weeks," he murmured, "Surely that has to be doable. I'm not fake dying though, no one's getting me in a coffin any time soon."

It took him a while to figure it out. Disappearing wasn't that easy when everything had a price but that was what he had to do. He needed to stay hidden until June fifteenth then find a way to contact someone in the security services, probably MI5, and share what Art Carew had told him. He could reference the letter Art had already sent. Oberon regretted not paying closer attention to Art, because all he had were the basics of Art's story. Even if he managed to stay out of the crosshairs long enough, there was still a huge risk that no one would believe him. *Gonna have to take my chances. A lot could happen in two weeks and surely the authorities can't be completely blind to this. They probably already know and I'll look like an idiot. I can deal with that.* "You wanted excitement, Obi. Should have kept your big trap shut."

Oberon assumed that there would be two sets of people looking for him — Art's enemies, already proven killers, and the police, who would want him for Art's murder. Keeping clear of them all was going to be a challenge. Oberon felt guilty that in a strange way he was excited about it. "I must be damaged. Well-paid boredom or a manhunt? What do I prefer? Fuck's sake, what an idiot." Still, when it came down to it, this was about saving his own neck. *Excellent motivation.*

Oberon's next thought was whether Art had left any clues in his limited belongings. He'd have to search the body. "Inspector Barnaby wouldn't approve," Oberon mumbled as he rifled through Art's pockets. His DNA would be all over the place anyway. The breast pocket was empty, and Art's wallet only held a few loose coins and a ten-pound note. In Art's trousers, Oberon found a miniature Swiss Army knife and a neatly folded handkerchief. There was no sign of the little black book where Art had scribbled his notes. "Maybe the murderer took it. That would make sense."

He stood up, disappointed, but noticed some drawers had been left slightly open in the sideboard, a mid-century Ercol piece that Oberon would have happily used for firewood but suited his absent landlord's taste. Art would never have left them open. He was meticulous, never leaving any trace of his daily activities around the flat. Someone must have been searching for something—maybe the notebook.

Oberon went around the flat and spotted signs that everything had been searched. A rudimentary attempt at putting things back the way they were had been made but the signs were there. He blamed his initial obliviousness on the shock of finding a dead body and a few glasses of wine. The buzz was wearing off quickly. Everything had been investigated—books had been shaken, drawers rifled through. The clothes in his wardrobe were out of place, suggesting all the pockets had been searched too. Oberon followed the trail but couldn't find any trace of the notebook. The killer hadn't found it on Art's body, so he assumed they had probably discovered it elsewhere.

He went back to his bed and grabbed his phone. He made sure it was in incognito mode then brought up a map of the British Isles, thinking that he needed to go somewhere as remote and isolated as possible. Working in inhospitable parts of the world had given him the skills he'd need to survive off the grid, but where to go? A city was out of the question with CCTV cameras on every other corner. He decided it would have to be Scotland. Sure there were other remote areas, but none big enough to get lost in for long enough. If he went to the Lakes or Snowdonia, he'd probably trip over a mountain rescue team saving some other poor sod. He had a strange, hybrid accent picked up over many years. He could take on Art's idea of being a travel blogger, but with a twist. Something closer to one of those survival programmes on TV. *That could work.* He decided on the Highlands, at least to start with.

A bit more searching gave him a location to aim for. The Knoydart peninsula boasted the UK mainland's most remote pub, a place called The Old Forge. There was a craggy coastline and one of Scotland's two hundred and eighty-two Munros, or mountains over three thousand feet, Ladair Bheinn. If he lost himself around there, he'd likely have only golden eagles and red deer for company. There were also only two routes in, from Mallaig on the passenger-only ferry, or a sixteen-kilometre hike from Kinloch Hourn.

He decided that the safest way to travel would be by train. The police would expect him to make a run for it straight away, so he'd leave them a few misleading clues that would meet their expectations. Using his British credit card, he bought a ferry ticket from Portsmouth to Le Havre and a flight from Stanstead to Agadir in Morocco. He still had a South African bank account that he guessed would take longer to trace. He used that to buy a ticket for the Caledonian Sleeper the following night. The train left Euston at eight-thirty and would get him to Fort William by ten o'clock the next morning. He booked a cabin for two passengers using the name of an old mining friend currently working in Chile, hoping it would add another layer of deception. All he had to do was figure out how to get away from the flat and set some false trails until he could board the sleeper.

He slept fitfully for two hours, plagued by dreams of being chased through unfamiliar landscapes, never able to get away from mysterious pursuers. There was an all-consuming sense of unleashed violence. By four o'clock, he gave up and got out of bed. The weather seemed to be on his side because it was bucketing down, the faint early light grey and murky. A few hopeful sparrows were attempting a dawn chorus with limited success. Oberon's guts twinged. He wasn't sure if that was a result of the previous night's drinking or the reckless plan he was about to carry out. It was tempting to leave everything to the police but he couldn't see how that would end well, either for him or for Kairos Doukas. *Stick with the plan, Obi.*

He dug out some of his outdoor gear, which had formed his regular wardrobe while working abroad. Limiting himself to a small pack, he stuffed it with a change of clothes, a minimal wash kit, Art's pocketknife and a compass. He put in his passport, hoping its absence from any police search might suggest an escape abroad. He had some cash but would get more before he boarded the train. Then he took a shower, shaved and got dressed.

By the time he moved to the kitchen, it was getting lighter outside, though the rain showed no signs of letting up. Despite his unsettled stomach, he forced himself to have breakfast. He poured cereal into a bowl and to his astonishment, Art's notebook tumbled out of the box with the cornflakes. The cereal went down a bit easier after that, and Oberon felt that luck might be on his side. He was going to need plenty of it for the next part of his plan to work.

He left his cereal dish on the draining board, wanting it to seem as if he'd left in a hurry then went back to his bedroom. In the back of his wardrobe, he found a set of stained orange overalls that had seen service in a range of different mines. He put them on over his clothes, then covered his light blond hair with a black woolly hat. He slipped on a pair of dark-framed glasses he sometimes used for close work then glanced at his reflection in the nearest mirror. "Well, it won't fool anyone who knows me well, but it should work for now."

He was counting on the timely arrival of the council bin men. It was collection day, and they were due any minute. After leaving his phone on his bedside table,

Oberon stuffed a lightweight waterproof jacket in the top of his pack, said a wry goodbye to Art Carew's lifeless corpse then made his way down the stairs to the building's basement. The dark, unheated space housed the communal bins and a bike store. The refuse guys would drag the huge, wheeled dumpsters outside to their compactor, and Oberon planned to help them. He hoped to blend in with the crew, who also wore bright orange safety gear. They moved fast and he doubted any of them would question a friendly resident giving them a hand.

He hung around in the shadows listening to the noise seeping into the basement from the street. He worried that Art's enemies may have made an anonymous call to the police alerting them to the body in Oberon's flat, but maybe they were waiting to see what he would do. Once he was clear, Oberon had decided he'd make the call himself. It wasn't right to leave Art there. He might already be 'dead' in the eyes of the world, but there was a huge difference between that and being left to decompose. Oberon shuddered. He was itching to get moving but today of all days, the refuse guys were running late. Six-thirty passed, then six-forty, and still they didn't come.

At six forty-seven Oberon heard the clanking and grinding of the compactor as it moved down the street. The crew were bantering with each other, yelling and joking above the racket of the truck.

Waking up the entire fucking street. For once, Oberon didn't mind. More people up and about early would help rather than hinder his disappearance. He shouldered his pack and when the roller door lifted, he was ready. He pretended that he'd just dropped the lid of the dumpster.

"All right, mate?" The refuse guy had a Polish accent and a big smile. "You done?" He didn't wait for an answer but put his weight behind the bin and wheeled it out onto the street. Oberon moved with him, keeping the bin between himself and the line of sight down the road. The crew in orange ignored him completely. The truck was already moving and Oberon walked alongside it until it turned the corner at the end of his street. He glanced back, spotting a homeless guy huddled in a doorway opposite his building. Two floors up in the same building, curtains twitched. Oberon watched for a minute or two, convinced that both observers were looking for him. There was no sign that his escape had been spotted. He shrugged and moved on, turning up his collar and hoping the rain would end soon.

He contemplated ditching his overalls but decided that hiding in plain sight might be smarter. He wasn't the only worker walking along in high vis clothing. He headed in the direction of Leadenhall, where construction of the building known as Cheesegrater 2 was under construction. As one of the biggest commercial building projects in London, it would be swarming with men and women dressed like him.

Close to the site, he ducked into a café with a group of other workers. He found a table towards the back where he could see the door and settled in to kill some time and dry off. The breathing space would give him time to plan his next move. His apparent success so far had given him an appetite and the smell of frying bacon was too good to resist. *Apparently escape efforts need more fuel than cereal alone.*

Chapter Three

Staying under the radar meant appearing like he belonged. Oberon had a leisurely breakfast then used the bathroom to change out of his overalls, which he balled up and left in the bin. He kept the hat on, worried that his hair was his most distinctive, easy-to-spot feature but got rid of his specs. Two doors down from the café was a charity shop with racks stuffed full of clothing. He went in and bought a cheap waterproof coat in a sludge-khaki colour. He didn't want to use his more expensive hiking waterproof until he needed it in Scotland because it was a more identifiable colour. He picked up another woollen hat at the same time so that he could swap it later. A cheap pair of dark sunglasses and a folding umbrella completed his purchases. Anything that kept his face from the proliferation of cameras on London's streets had to be worthwhile.

After that, he did his best to blend in with the crowds, interspersing periods of walking with bus rides in random directions. He spent some time in Hyde Park then bought a ticket at the cinema, choosing the biggest screen where there were several exits. The time passed quicker than he expected. He kept an eye out for anyone that might be following him, but he wasn't an expert in covert surveillance. Every now and again he caught someone's eye or imagined seeing the same person reflected in a store window, but he put it down to his overstressed imagination.

The weather had caused some transport delays and when he got to Euston, the concourse was packed with soggy, disgruntled travellers. He used the bathrooms to change his appearance again, dumping the umbrella and cheap coat in a lost property box. He didn't have to worry about the rain in the station. He also swapped hats. He bought a cheap pre-paid mobile phone at a kiosk and loaded it with credit, being sure to pay cash, then checked the departure boards and found that the Caledonian Sleeper was at the platform and boarding had opened. He walked alongside a woman struggling with a trolley load of luggage and two small children.

"You need a hand? I'm travelling light."

She gave him a grateful nod. "Lifesaver. If you could push the trolley that would be fantastic. I couldn't manage a buggy as well and wrangling these two is a job."

"No problem." Oberon pushed the trolley to her allocated carriage then lifted her baggage onto the train. She got on and he hoisted the two giggling kids in to her, then climbed on board. His sleeping compartment was at the other end of the train, but he didn't intend to go there right away. He said goodbye to the harassed mother then made his way to one of the lounge cars. In a nod to tradition, there were newspapers in a rack on the wall. He grabbed one and browsed the headlines. It was the usual doom and gloom. England's cricket team were losing against

India. There was flooding in various parts of the country. Politics was becoming increasingly polarized. There was nothing, however, about a murder near Langham Place.

Oberon had a pen in his pack and spent a while puzzling over the cryptic crossword, quietly observing his fellow passengers as they explored the train. The regular travellers were easy to spot, moving with purpose. Those for whom the sleeper was a novelty were more aimless, oohing at the facilities. So far, there was nobody who worried him.

"Hey, you mind if I join you? There aren't many seats." Oberon eyed the man who spoke. He was maybe in his late twenties, had eyes that were a darker shade of blue then Oberon's, and hair a glossy dark brown. He was clean shaven and Oberon could see the hint of a tattoo beneath the neckline of his T-shirt. Something small and colourful. Oberon guessed it might be the tail of a dolphin or a butterfly wing. His navy T-shirt had a rainbow on it and underneath, a slogan in capital letters that read *Sounds gay. I'm in*. He was slim, maybe five feet nine or ten, and pretty. Very pretty.

Oberon gestured at the empty seat at his table. "Help yourself. Like the T-shirt."

The young man gave him a calculating look. "Really?"

"Hey, between us, we must be fulfilling the gay quota on this train."

"That's more than fabulous. I'm Syd, with a y."

"Of course you are." Oberon grinned. "Richard."

"So you go by Dick, Dickie…?"

"Richard. Richard is fine. Call me Dick and you and I will have a problem."

Syd beamed. "We are so gonna be besties. Is this your first time?"

I have a first class brat on my hands here. "I've been on sleeper trains before, just not in this country. I'm guessing you're *not* a virgin."

"Hardly, I'm twenty-seven. Oh, I've also been on the train a few times before."

Oberon shook his head. Syd was definitely going to make the journey a lot more interesting.

"Are you married? Significant other? Secretly a monk who's taken a vow of chastity?"

"You need a fucking spanking. I'm single."

"Me too. And yes, I probably do. Are you offering?" Syd batted his thick lashes shamelessly.

"We've known each other for all of two minutes, do you not think that's moving a little fast?"

"Hey, I like to grab opportunities when they present themselves. There's no crime in that. You're very easy on the eyes, though I'm not sure about the hat."

Oberon pulled the beanie off then ran a hand through his hair. "Forgot I was wearing it."

Syd licked his lips. "Well, I really wish I had a cabin instead of a recliner. The things I'd let you do to me..."

"How about we start with coffee?"

"I guess we could do that. I'll get the first round if you save my seat." Syd left his overnight bag in his chair then made his way towards the buffet car.

Oberon watched him go, admiring the sway of his hips. *Little sod is wiggling that ass on purpose, I know he is.* Needing a less tempting distraction, he pulled out Art's notebook and studied it. It was filled with jottings, a lot of numbers, with a few names scattered throughout. Rownham, Hickman and Frobisher appeared several times, Ariadne was there too. Oberon was certain that Art had never done anything without a reason, and was pretty sure there had to be a cypher hidden in the scribbles. *That would definitely fit his conspiracy theories.* Oberon enjoyed all kinds of puzzles and hoped he'd be able to crack any secret code. This one looked like it might use numbers to represent letters, but anyone with a working brain cell could figure those out. He didn't think Art would have settled for something so basic, so he focused on the printed words. *You can make a pretty good numerical cypher if you have a key word which gives you the sequence of the letters.*

He stared at the notebook for almost half an hour before wondering where Syd had got to. He put the book in his pack and was about to go looking when Syd appeared at the end of the carriage. He was carrying two big cups of coffee, steam rising from them.

"Sorry! Bet you thought I'd ghosted you or something. The queue was ridiculous. I thought we were gonna get to Scotland before I got back to you."

"I was about to come look for you."

Syd gave him a disarming smile. "I'm glad I made an impression."

"Oh, it wasn't you. I just desperately needed that coffee."

"Liar, liar, pants on fire!" Syd sat down. "It's always the same. Train leaves and there's a mass stampede for hot drinks and snacks. The line was out of the carriage."

"You make this journey a lot then?"

"Yeah. I loathe flying, the motorways are purgatory and I have family in Fort William. My grandma. This is the least bad option and there's usually some poor sod I can bore with my company."

"I'm not bored yet." Oberon sipped his coffee. "This isn't bad for a train."

"These people are trapped on here overnight. Can you imagine the riots if the coffee was undrinkable?"

Oberon chuckled. "Good point."

"So what about you, why are you heading north?"

"Bit of a mental health break, I guess. You know how it is, stressful job, needed a change. Not quite a mid-life crisis, but I wanted to do something new. Gonna try some blogging about wild hiking and remote places."

"Cool! I mean, I don't think the outdoors bit would be for me…too much damp plays havoc with my hair and I have a love-hate relationship with creepy-crawlies…but blogging, vlogging, whatever, would be fun."

They talked for a while about the bits of Scotland Syd knew and his suggestions for places Oberon might travel to. Syd was easy to talk to and a good listener. It didn't escape Oberon's notice that he talked less about himself but there was plenty of time to get to know him. By eleven, after his long, stressful day, Oberon was flagging. He tried to hide a yawn.

"Bed for me, I think."

"Yeah, it's getting late. You want to get breakfast together?"

Oberon made a snap decision. "How about you give up your recliner and join me in my compartment? Then we'd be sure not to miss each other in the morning."

"You mean, sleep with you?" Syd widened his eyes.

"The innocent act won't work on me. You're more transparent than a sheet of glass. Yes, sleep… eventually."

"We barely know each other."

"Do we need to? I'm not proposing marriage and you said you liked to seize the moment."

Syd laughed. "I did, didn't I? Carpe diem and all that. Lead me to your lair. There's not much I won't do to avoid an uncomfortable, sleepless night."

"Then let's go explore your limits, shall we?" Oberon got to his feet. Some no-strings fun was exactly what he needed.

Oberon's compartment proved to be nothing like he imagined — which was something from *Murder on the Orient Express*, all dark wood and art deco light fittings. It was compact and modern and had everything a traveller could need for an overnight journey, including a comfortable double bed. There was a tiny bathroom with a shower, sink and toilet, and even the lights were dimmable. Syd had to try every button and knob, as delighted as a child with a new toy.

"This is all so cool!" He played with the TV, flicking through the channel choices.

"I'm going to take a shower," Oberon said, smiling at Syd's enthusiasm.

Syd peered around the en suite's door. "We'd have to be contortionists for us both to fit in there. I mean I *am* flexible but…"

"Make yourself comfortable. I won't be long." Oberon took his toothbrush from his pack then shoved the bag well under the bed. He had his wallet and passport on him, so there was nothing in the pack to give away his true identity should Syd get curious, and Art's notebook would be meaningless. The hot water felt great and when he was done, Oberon wrapped a towel around his hips before padding into the cabin. He left his clothes on hooks behind the bathroom door, documents in a zipped inside pocket.

Syd was sprawled on the bed clad only in his underwear. His very brief underwear. He rolled onto his side and gave Oberon an appreciative look.

"Wow."

"You took me at my word then?"

"The bed is comfy and I run hot. You don't mind, do you?"

"Only that you left an item of clothing on."

Syd grinned. "Lose the towel and I'll lose the shorts."

"Pushy brat."

"We have one night. I want to make the most of it. Give me a minute." Syd made a dive for the bathroom. When he emerged he was naked, his slender cock erect. The tattoo Oberon had spotted proved to be a colourful butterfly.

Oberon had removed the towel. He admired Syd's lean physique. *Fuck, he's gorgeous.* "You work out?"

"I like to run. Don't do gyms, too stinky. You?"

"Tore up my knee a few months back so I haven't got back to running yet. I've been swimming a lot, and walking."

Syd licked his lips. "It looks good on you."

"Thanks. You too. Uh, I don't have any condoms," Oberon said. "I wasn't expecting to hook up on a train."

"I do. I wasn't either, but I like to be prepared." Syd delved in his bag and dug out some condoms, which he tossed on the bed. "I have lube too." He sounded jubilant and waved the bottle like a trophy.

"Quite the Boy Scout."

"Fortunate one of us is. Quit talking, Richard. I really want to suck your dick."

For a moment, Oberon forgot he was using a false name. He covered his confusion by plumping a pillow, then stretched out on the bed. "I'm not stopping you."

Considering how long his dry spell had been, Oberon thought he deserved an award for how long he held out before he came. Syd sucked dick like a vacuum cleaner. He also had no gag reflex. Nor did he object when Oberon grabbed his hair and held him in place. Oberon's orgasm was a thing of beauty.

"Holy crap, you're good at that." Oberon felt drained and limp. "Give me a minute and I'll return the favour."

"Take your time. I want you in me… If that's okay?"

"It's more than okay. Might need more than a minute in that case though."

Syd flopped onto the bed, resting his head on Oberon's chest. "I took you as a toppy, likes-to-be-in-control type."

"Pretty much. It's been a while though."

"Not feeling the London scene?"

"I was talking about this to a friend the other day." *Seems like a lifetime ago.* "Cruising the clubs isn't my thing anymore. Must be getting old."

"You're not old! There are better ways to meet people anyway. I like a bit of connection, which I think we have. No strings fun is great, but I need a spark at least."

"Yeah. I'm the same. I guess I'll settle down one day. Not sure where, though. I thought it would be England but who knows?"

"You've travelled then?"

"I work in mining exploration. The job involves lots of travel but most places I go aren't exactly sun, sea and shenanigans territory."

"I'll bet. More mosquito repellent and weaponry?"

"Something like that."

"I can see why you need to get away and decompress for a while."

"Clean air, exercise… I'm looking forward to it. I just hope the weather is kind to me. Wild camping in the pouring rain isn't fun."

"Wild camping…ugh. Torture even in the sunshine."

Oberon drifted into a doze with a smile on his face. It had been some time since he'd shared a bed and Syd's warmth and closeness was nice. He got a lot more alert very fast when Syd wrapped a hand around his cock. He hardened instantly.

Holy fuck!

"Nice girth. I like a bit of stretch," Syd said.

"Did you just critique my cock?"

"Twelve points from the UK jury."

"Thanks. I think."

There was a rustle of foil and then Syd was slipping a condom over Oberon's erection. He popped open the lube then applied a liberal coating.

"Topping from the bottom, Syd?"

"Just reminding you I'm here." Syd got onto his hands and knees, disturbing the bedding. Oberon kicked it to one side. Syd reached for his hole and started prepping himself. "Is this a big enough hint?"

"Jesus."

Syd laughed. "Sticky hands." He grabbed a wad of tissues, cleaned his fingers off then tossed them onto the floor. Oberon got behind him and Syd wiggled his butt.

"Ready, willing and able."

Oberon tested the water by giving him a couple of smacks. Syd moaned, the sound soft and low. "Ooh yes. In me."

Oberon shifted into position. "Say please."

"Please! Pretty please with marshmallows on."

"You sure you're ready?" Oberon didn't have a problem delivering pain when it was invited, but Syd was an unknown quantity and he didn't want to hurt him.

"I'd tell you if I wasn't."

Oberon pressed the head of his gloved cock to Syd's hole. Syd fisted the sheet and Oberon pushed into him. It was a tight fit. Oberon took it slow and Syd wiggled, encouraging him deeper.

"Needy boy."

"Less talking, more fucking!"

"There'll be more spanking if you're not careful." Oberon kept up a steady rhythm and Syd moved with him, muscles rippling. He reached for his cock, jacking it slowly at first and then with frantic motions. He came with a yell, body shaking, a sheen of perspiration glistening on his skin.

"Ooh, yeah. So good."

Having come once already, the urgency had gone for Oberon. He took a measured pace, enjoying the grip of Syd's body and the needy noises that came from him. On the edge, Oberon pushed deeper. His orgasm this time rolled through him like distant thunder, languorous but still powerful.

They panted in unison before Oberon carefully withdrew. He went to the bathroom to dispose of the condom while Syd snuggled beneath the covers. Leaning on the sink, Oberon contemplated his reflection. His eyes were bright and cheeks flushed. *Considering the circumstances, Wycherley, that was probably not your best move, but fuck, it was fun.* He did a quick clean up then went back to bed. Syd appeared to be sleeping but as soon as Oberon slipped beneath the covers, he wriggled closer.

"Cuddler, huh?" Oberon asked.

"You mind?"

"No."

That was the extent of their conversation for the rest of the night and Oberon slept more soundly than he had any right to.

Chapter Four

Any potential awkwardness the following morning was dealt with by mutual wake-up blow jobs. By the time Oberon and Syd had left their cabin and breakfast was done, the train was pulling into Fort William. That meant a walk to his grandma's for Syd and a wait for Oberon until the next train to Mallaig.

"You know, there's a decent café not far from the station," Syd said. "How about I buy you a coffee and keep you company until your next train gets in?"

Oberon could think of worse ways to spend the time. "Sounds good, if you're sure you have time."

"Of course. Granny knows I'm easily distracted."

"Okay then, but it's my turn to buy." Oberon shouldered his pack and followed Syd through the ticket barrier.

The Croft Café was only five minutes' walk away. Inside it was warm and welcoming. The array of cakes on offer was tempting but Oberon was still full from breakfast. He settled for a flat white, which came with a piece of homemade shortbread on the side. Syd had the same. They settled at a corner table and Oberon people watched while Syd scoffed both pieces of shortbread.

"I'll give you my number," Syd said. "Then you can call me when you come back this way or, you know, if you need anything. Not that there's likely to be any reception out in the wilds, so try not to trip over a haggis. That wouldn't be a fun way to go. They can be vicious."

"Funny. Don't give up the day job. What is that, by the way?"

"Promise you won't laugh?"

"Why? Are you going to tell me you're an accountant?"

"Worse. I'm a civil servant."

"That's…"

"A conversation killer, I know. I wish I could say I was something sexy like a computer games designer or paramedic."

"Someone has to run the country," Oberon said, picturing Syd in a bowler hat and nothing else. He fought back a laugh. "I'd love your number. I don't know how long it'll be before I'm back this way though. I'll give you mine too." Oberon gave Syd the number of the cheap burner phone he'd bought and Syd called him so he could save the contact.

"It's a shame you can't stay here overnight," Syd said. "There's a steam train that does the Mallaig route called the Jacobite — it's a spectacular way to go, especially over the Glenfinnan viaduct."

"Maybe the timings will work out on the return journey. Does the modern train follow the same route?"

"Yeah, it goes via Glenfinnan and Arisaig. That could be something for your blog — you can take a boat from Arisaig to the Small Isles."

"The Small Isles?"

"Part of the Inner Hebrides. The four main islands are Canna, Rùm, Eigg and Muck."

"Oh right, I've heard of them. Are they all still inhabited?"

"Those four are, yes. There are some smaller islands as well. Sanday is separated from Canna by a narrow tidal channel; Eilean Chathastail is near Eigg and Eilean nan Each is near the north coast of Muck. There are some skerries too."

"And skerries are…?

"Rocky islets."

"You know the geography well."

"Spent most Easter breaks up here when I was growing up. My grandma used to live in Arisaig but moved here a while back. Summers were usually in the Lake District. I went to school in England, hence no Scottish accent."

Syd chattered away about other places Oberon could explore and it wasn't long before he had to go to catch his train.

Syd gave him a hug. "Don't forget me, Richard. I don't even know your last name!"

"Or me yours. You're unforgettable. I hope we meet again, Syd." Oberon didn't offer a name. Another lie didn't sit well with him. Outside the café, he gave Syd a brief but intense kiss then walked away without looking back.

The train to Mallaig was busy, crammed with a mix of tourists and locals. Oberon pretended to nap as far as Arisaig then kept a discreet eye on who was getting on and off. Through the window he spotted a man on the platform who seemed out of place in a dark suit and tie, but Oberon couldn't tell if he boarded the train. *He could be going to a funeral or be dressed for business I suppose. Mustn't be paranoid.*

Oberon's end of the carriage was packed full of farmers fresh from a morning market. Their talk was all about stock prices, subsidies and the apparently outrageous price of feed. The government was cursed creatively and often. The conversation was fuelled by the contents of a hip flask, which was doing the rounds. Oberon declined the offer of a swig and was happily ignored from then on. He stared out of the window and admired the spectacular view as the impressive height of the viaduct gave way to wooded glens then to open moorland, shimmering lochs, and snow-capped hills to the north. *Still snow on the tops at this time of the year. Better not venture too high or I'll freeze.*

He planned to catch the ferry from Mallaig to Inverie, the main village on the Knoydart peninsula. He hoped to find a place to stay for the night before hiking into more remote country. After leaving the train in Mallaig he used cash to buy some supplies and invested in a one-man tent and good quality sleeping bag, both of which he strapped to his pack. A helpful lady at the tourist information centre gave him directions to a bed and breakfast two miles outside the village but first he used a public phone booth to call the Crimestoppers information line. A direct call to the police would be traced. He left a cryptic message about the possibility of a body at his address before setting off along a road that wound past a few houses before heading over the moors.

It was a gorgeous spring afternoon, with every hill showing as clear as a cut amethyst, purple with heather. The air had the boggy smell of marshes, but it was fresh and clean. Oberon took a deep breath and his mood lifted. *Anyone would think I'm out for a fun hike, not wanted by the police.* He wondered if Art's body had already been discovered. *But that would only have happened if it suited Art's enemies. My enemies now, so more than likely.* His plans were vague at best but he was glad to be away from London and more in control of his own destiny.

He spotted a sturdy hazel branch under a hedge, perfect as a walking stick, and grabbed it before veering off the road onto a narrow track, barely wide enough for a tractor. It followed the course of a babbling stream so clear that Oberon could see multi-coloured pebbles scattered like jewels along its bed.

He was getting hungry by the time he reached the B&B—a cosy cottage nestled beside a waterfall. A woman stood at the door. She was grey-haired with weathered skin, dressed in jeans and a brightly coloured sweater.

"Maeve at the tourist office called to let me know you might be heading this way," she said, as Oberon approached. "You must be Richard."

"News travels fast around here." Oberon grinned.

"Aye. Everybody knows everything about everyone in the main but don't worry, Maeve's not a gossip." She extended a hand, which proved to be dry and warm when Oberon shook it. She had a strong, steady grip. "Aileen Mackintosh."

"So I'm good for a bed for the night?"

"Aye, you are. There's the one room in the attic. Will you be wanting a meal?"

"If it's not too much trouble, that would be fantastic. I'm starving."

"Come away in then." Inside, she pointed out the stairs. "Turn right at the top and take the narrow stairs.

The room has a shower and basin if you want to freshen up. Supper will be ready in an hour."

The shower was welcome, the meal even more so. In the cottage kitchen, Aileen served up a plate of the best ham and eggs Oberon had ever tasted. The homemade, crusty bread that came with it was sublime.

"Do your guests ever want to leave, Aileen? This food is amazing." Oberon sipped from a mug of hot tea after finishing his food.

"Go on with you." Aileen smiled. "There are freshly baked scones for afters."

"I may have died and gone to heaven."

It was getting dark when Aileen's husband came in. He was a giant of a man whose hand engulfed Oberon's when he said hello. He ate the same meal, giving Aileen appreciative smiles. Neither of them pried into Oberon's plans, instead talking about farming. Angus Mackintosh had been to the same market as the farmers on Oberon's train and he was on a mission to update his wife with all the local gossip.

By ten o' clock, Oberon was nodding off in his chair, and excused himself to bed. He slept undisturbed by dreams and didn't wake until noises from the floor below told him the household was getting up. By eight he had devoured an enormous breakfast, settled his bill and was striding out onto the moors. He hoped his efforts at subterfuge would mean that the police would assume he had fled abroad. *It'll take them a while to figure out I didn't take a boat or plane, even if they suspect me of Art's murder. It'll take them even longer to identify me as a passenger on the sleeper train.* Anxiety still gnawed at him so he took an abrupt decision to return to Mallaig in order to get hold of the morning paper. He hid his pack beneath a distinctive cluster of rocks then jogged back to the village.

Skirting the side of a high hill, he tested his knee's resilience, which was holding up well on the rough terrain. Nesting curlews and plovers cried out all around, and the greener pastures by the streams were dotted with young lambs. In the distance, he spotted a train pulling into the station. He reached it just as a crowd of passengers was making its way out and had to queue at the kiosk for a copy of *The Scotsman*.

With the paper in hand, he sat on a bench on the platform, pretending to wait for a train. There were two columns about what was being called the Portland Place Murder. There was a brief mention of Oberon as the tenant of the flat, but nothing more. There was no picture and no hint that he was a suspect, though that would be implied. *They'll definitely be on my trail.*

Another train was pulling in, brakes screeching, so Oberon hid behind the newspaper. Three men got off, one of them in police uniform, and headed for the station master's office. *They must be the local police, stirred up by the Met. How the hell have they made it here so fast?* Oberon left the paper on the bench then made his way back to the road he had followed the previous day. *You're making assumptions, idiot. They could be here for any reason.* The uneasy feeling in his gut told him otherwise and he regretted the time his detour had taken.

He retrieved his pack then began walking with more urgency. He was in a wide semicircle of moorland, with a river as the radius and high hills forming the northern circumference. There was no sign or sound of human activity, only the splashing of water and the cries of curlews, but for the first time Oberon felt the terror of being hunted. It wasn't the police that worried him most but those who believed he knew Art's secret and would want to silence him. He was sure their pursuit would be better resourced and relentless. He didn't want to consider what might happen when, or if, they found him.

The men at the station had spooked him. He looked back, but saw nothing of immediate concern. Nevertheless, a sense of impending danger propelled him to run. Crouching low in the runnels of a bog, he ran until his heaving chest forced him to stop. He had reached the top of a steep slope and flung himself onto his belly, panting, on the ridge. Every sound seemed amplified — the rustle of wind through the grass, the distant calls of birds, and the rush of blood in his ears. He strained to hear any signs of pursuit, but there was only silence. He forced himself to calm down, reminding himself that panic could be as deadly as any pursuer. *Stop being so fucking paranoid. You'll wear yourself out with all this moronic rushing about.*

From his vantage-point Oberon could scan the entire moor to the railway line and beyond, where green fields replaced the purple expanse of heather. "Nothing, there's nothing. Calm down." He reassured himself, his gaze sweeping the view to the east where shallow green valleys were dotted with fir plantations and the faint lines of roads. He took off his pack then flopped onto his back in the heather. The sky above was clear and blue. "Oh fuck," he muttered, his heart pounding.

Low down in the valley, a black speck was climbing into the air. Oberon was as certain as if he'd been told by the operator that the drone was looking for him, and it didn't belong to the police.

He burrowed into the heather and watched intently. The drone flew low along the hilltops, then began to circle over the valley he'd just crossed. It hovered there for what felt like an eternity before rising high into the air and flying away back to the south.

"Fuck, this isn't good," Oberon murmured. His mind raced. This wasn't just a simple manhunt — whoever was after him had access to advanced technology. He had to be smarter, faster, and more cautious. He hadn't considered being tracked from the air and now the area he'd chosen to escape to didn't seem so great. The heather-covered hills didn't provide enough cover from enemies in the sky. "Need to find somewhere better." He scanned the view and decided on the distant woods.

Keeping low made for painfully slow progress. The undergrowth tugged at his clothes, and every movement felt arduous. He had to abandon his stick which kept catching in the scrub. About six in the evening he came off the moor to a narrow ribbon of road that followed a valley. As he followed it, fields gave way to open grassland and the glen reached a plateau. The road swung over a low stone bridge, and leaning on the parapet was a man perhaps a few years younger than Oberon.

He wore wire-framed glasses and held a book in one hand. He jumped as Oberon approached, clearly surprised by the appearance of a stranger.

"Sorry! I didn't mean to startle you," Oberon said, trying to sound casual and not worthy of suspicion.

"I was miles away. I don't see many people up here," the man replied with a lopsided grin. He gestured at a house beyond the bridge. "I'm renting that place while I work on a book."

"Needed peace and quiet, eh?" Oberon asked. "It's a great spot."

"I thought I did, but I'm getting a bit stir crazy to be honest. How about you?"

Oberon launched into his well-rehearsed story about seeking a change of pace and travel blogging. The scent of wood smoke and cooking drifted his way and his stomach rumbled.

"I'm Ed. Ed Burns. Nice to meet you," the man said, extending his hand.

Oberon shook it. "Likewise. Richard Van Den Broek. And no, before you ask, nobody calls me Dick."

Ed chuckled. "That's a mercy. Where are you heading?"

"Nowhere in particular at the moment. I was thinking of finding a place to camp for the night. Do you know of anywhere good around here?"

"How about you join me instead? There's a decent spare room, a warm fire and I have enough dinner for two."

"I wouldn't want to impose," Oberon replied, not wanting to seem too eager.

"You'd be doing me a favour. I'm sick of my own company and a bit of conversation would be welcome."

Oberon took off his pack then had a look over the bridge at the lively stream below. "The water here is so clear."

"Isn't it? I came up here from London and I swear my lungs didn't know what hit them."

"You're young to be a writer," Oberon observed.

"My father died a year ago and left me the family business, a chain of pubs. Running them wasn't my choice of profession, so I sold up." Ed blushed. "I want to write books. I've given myself a year to see if I can finish something. After that, who knows? I want to travel. Have adventures."

Oberon looked at the house standing golden in the sunset against the hills. "I've travelled a bit. Adventure isn't only found in deserts and jungles. You could be closer to it than you think."

"I want a life measured in first steps on foreign soils and deep breaths in brand new seas I want a life measured in Welcome Signs, each stamped with a different name, borders marked with metal and paint. Show me the streets that don't know the music of my meandering feet, and I will play their song upon them."

"Did you write that?" Oberon asked, impressed.

"I wish! No, it's by an American poet called Tyler Knott Gregson. But I see your point about the possibility of adventure being around every corner."

"You're a romantic."

"Aren't we all, at heart?"

Oberon couldn't, in all conscience, accept Ed's hospitality without being more truthful. He decided it was worth the risk. "I'd love to stay but I've been a bit economical with the truth."

Ed pushed his glasses up his nose, a slight frown creasing his forehead. "You're not an escaped axe murderer, are you?"

"Not quite." Oberon chuckled, appreciating Ed's attempt at humour. "I'll tell you a bit…maybe you can make a novel out of it. Then if you want me to leave, I'll head off and it'll be up to you to decide what to do."

Sitting on the bridge in the soft evening light, Oberon began to tell Ed what was really going on. It was mostly true, though he altered some details and put himself in Art's place. "To cut a long, painful story short, I was working in mining in a part of Africa where the law doesn't hold much sway. I stumbled into a smuggling ring transporting blood diamonds into Europe and had to make a run for it. I was followed across half a continent and across the sea as far as London." Oberon paused, picturing Art's body. "I was stupid. I begged a bed from a friend but the people after me were closer than I thought. They mistook my friend for me and now he's dead."

"Oh my God!" Ed seemed transfixed, his eyes wide.

"These people aren't afraid of the law and have a long reach. The Met police think I'm a murderer and the smugglers are still after me. I'm here because I need to stay in front of them until the British authorities work out the truth."

"Bloody hell!" Ed whispered, drawing his breath in sharply, "It's like a movie storyline. You'd probably be played by Gerard Butler or Daniel Craig."

"You believe me?" Oberon asked. "I'm not sure I would, in your shoes."

"Of course I do, it's too far-fetched to be a lie. Not sure it's the whole truth though."

"If I told you everything you wouldn't be safe," Oberon replied, his tone serious. He then told Ed about the drone. "I think they're off my track for the moment, but I daren't move for a while. Are you still happy to give me a bed?"

"If you're in that much danger, you need a safe place to stay. I've got room and, frankly, I could use the company. If you give me more material about your adventures and let me use it, you can stay as long as you like." He bumped his hip against Oberon's. "You think maybe you should get inside out of sight?"

They walked to the house and as Oberon went through the porch, he spotted movement in the sky.

Silhouetted against the blue was the drone. "Nice timing. The bloody thing can't see through stone."

Ed ushered him inside. "Quick. You weren't kidding, were you?"

"I wish I was."

"You can have the room at the back of the house," Ed said. "It has a great outlook...not that you'll be interested in the view or anything."

"Thanks." After a day walking and running, tiredness was overtaking Oberon's willingness to be sociable. "I can't tell you how much I appreciate this."

"Dump your pack and I'll get food on the table."

They ate in the kitchen. The scent of cooking Oberon had noticed outside had come from a tasty stew Ed had put together in a slow cooker. He served it with hunks of crusty bread.

"This is fantastic," Oberon said.

"Honestly, I'm a terrible cook. The slow cooker is a godsend. I just lob stuff in there and it produces a meal, like magic."

Oberon nodded around another mouthful. "Whatever works."

"I use the back room as a study," Ed explained. "There are just the two bedrooms and a shared bathroom upstairs. Feel free to have a soak in the bath if you want to. After what you've been through, I expect you want some alone time and there's loads of hot water. The cottage isn't on the power grid but there's a good generator."

"You're kind and perceptive. Must be your writer's eye," Oberon remarked with a hint of admiration.

"It's the most excitement I've had since I came up here." Ed opened a bottle of merlot. He poured them both a generous glass. "Do you have anyone special worrying about you?"

"No," Oberon replied, taking a sip of the wine. "I did meet a guy on the train…if I wasn't in such a sticky situation, I'd definitely call him. How about you?"

"Haven't found the right girl yet. Or boy," Ed said with a shrug. "I'm not in any hurry, but I do know you should grab chances when they come along."

"You sound like Syd. He had the same philosophy."

"There's a landline phone in the other room if you want to call your man. There's bugger all mobile reception around here. I think you should."

"You could be right." Oberon took his wine and ventured into Ed's study. The room was a testament to a writer's life, with books and papers heaped everywhere. The computer sat on the desk, humming quietly, and an old phone rested in a docking station beside it. "Haven't seen one of these in a while," Oberon said to himself. He pulled out his mobile to look up Syd's number, feeling a sudden rush of nerves. He dialled the number and waited. Finally, there was a click, and a familiar voice answered.

"Hello?"

"Syd, it's Richard. We met on the train."

"Are you calling me for phone sex because I'm so up for that?"

"Uh, no, and is that always your opening line after hello?"

"Not for everyone. Are you missing me already?"

"A bit. Is that weird?"

"Nope, I'm a memorable, loveable person."

"Well…"

"Okay, I'm like a bread roll, yummy but leaves crumbs everywhere."

"Oh my God."

"Are you having fun out there in the wilds?"

"It's beautiful country. I guess I was a bit lonely. I wanted to hear your voice."

"You're just a big 'ole marshmallow, aren't you? You want me to come join you?"

"I thought you hated the outdoors."

"I do, but for you I could make an exception."

"I wouldn't subject you to that. Can I call you again though?"

"Oh yeah, and next time bring your A game because I'll be expecting at least one orgasm, maybe two."

"Such a brat."

"You know it." Syd made kissy noises down the phone.

"Yeah, not doing that."

Syd snickered. "Okay, I'm gonna go entertain my dick for a while."

"Make sure it's me you're thinking about."

"Yes, Sir."

Syd's voice was so sultry, Oberon couldn't decide if he was still kidding around. Being called Sir gave him tingles in lots of interesting places.

"Like that, don't you? Going now."

"Oh my…" Oberon rang off before Syd could make more sex noises. He shook his head. Talking to Syd was like therapy. Considering how short a connection they'd had, he'd made a big impression. Oberon was touched about how happy Syd had sounded to get the call and how keen he was that they get back together. He rejoined Ed with a smile on his face.

"Did you get through?" Ed asked.

"Yeah, I did. Thanks for that," Oberon said, sinking back into his chair. "You were right, it was good to hear his voice."

Ed nodded. "Sometimes, just knowing someone out there cares makes all the difference."

"So, tell me more about your book," Oberon said, keen to shift the focus and learn more about Ed's passion project.

Ed's eyes lit up, and he launched into a description of his historical novel, the excitement in his voice palpable. Oberon listened, grateful for the distraction and the sense of normalcy it brought. The fire crackled softly, casting soft shadows on the walls. Oberon felt a strange sense of calm despite the chaos of his life. Here, in this remote house with a new friend, he'd found a brief respite.

After a while, fatigue caught up with him. He excused himself and made his way to the guest bedroom. The bed was comfortable but sleep didn't come easily and he tossed and turned for some time. He had hoped to dream about Syd but instead, when he did eventually fall asleep, he was haunted by visions of mysterious enemies closing in on him, faceless and threatening. Always getting closer.

The following morning as they shared a breakfast of porridge and toast, Oberon asked Ed to do him a favour.

"Do you have transport? This porridge is fabulous, by the way."

"Thanks, it's made with cream and local honey and yes, I do. I have a motorbike for short trips and a car in the garage around the back. Why? Do you need something?"

"Would you mind running into Mallaig and picking up the morning paper? I'd like to see if there's any update in the coverage of the murder."

"Sure. I need a few supplies anyway. I'll take the bike," Ed agreed.

"Keep your eyes open, Ed. Look out for anyone who seems out of place and if you spot the drone, ignore it. I don't want anyone thinking you're involved in my problems."

"I'll be careful," Ed assured him. "Help yourself to anything you need from the kitchen and if you could keep the fire going, that would be great. It gets a bit chilly in here even at this time of year — the walls are so thick."

"Sure." Oberon watched as Ed prepared to leave. The motorbike roared to life and Ed sped away into the early morning mist. Once he'd disappeared from view, Oberon cleaned up the breakfast things then stoked the fire. He retrieved Art's notebook from his bag then settled into a comfortable chair by the fire. He immersed himself in Art's cryptic notes and waited.

Ed was back in less than two hours but there was nothing in the paper that wasn't a repeat of the previous day's coverage.

"Don't you think it's a bit strange that the story isn't bigger?" Ed asked, handing the paper to Oberon.

"It is a bit odd," Oberon agreed, skimming the main stories. "I'm surprised they're not splashing my face around by now but they don't mention my name. Perhaps they've realised I'm being framed."

"Or it's too soon to come to conclusions," Ed suggested.

"That's more likely," Oberon conceded. "Did you see anything odd in the village?"

"No, it was as sleepy as usual. Perhaps they've given up and moved on."

Oberon wasn't convinced. He shrugged. "I can hope."

Ed nodded and headed to his study to get some work done, leaving Oberon to return to the notebook. He'd decided that Art had used a numerical cypher, and was getting closer to working it out. "The problem is the key word," he muttered. "It could be one of millions." He stared into the fire, hoping for inspiration from the flames. In his head he replayed the conversations he'd had with Art. The name Julia Kensington flashed across his memory. Art had said she was the key. "Different context, but I wouldn't put it past him to have snuck me a clue. Sneaky son of a... It has to be worth a try."

It worked. He applied the name to the cypher. The first five letters gave him the position of the vowels. A was J, the tenth letter of the alphabet, represented by X in the cypher. E was U=XXI, and so on. The surname Kensington gave him the numerals for the principal consonants. He scribbled the solution on a piece of paper then started to read Art's notes. He was so engrossed in decoding Art's words he didn't notice Ed slip into the room until he spoke in an urgent whisper.

"Richard." Ed's voice was low and tense.

"What is it?"

"I think we have company. There's a car outside. I spotted it driving up the road. Two men, wearing suits. I'm not expecting anyone and they don't look like they're from the village." He gestured towards the stairs. "Make yourself scarce."

Oberon gathered his things then headed up to his room. His window was on the wrong side of the house to observe anything so he had no choice but to sit and wait for Ed to signal that the coast was clear.

Five minutes felt like an hour. Oberon kept away from the window, wary of being seen by anyone who might be watching from the hillside. He breathed a sigh of relief when Ed finally slipped into the room.

"You're looking far too excited," Oberon said, amused by Ed's eager expression.

"Sorry. There were two of them," Ed explained. "They asked if I'd seen a hiker around here. They had an accurate description of you and claimed they needed to get hold of you urgently because of a family emergency. They said you were called Oberon Wycherley though."

"Ah, about that..."

"Don't worry about it. If I were you, I'd be using a false name too."

"You're amazing, Ed. What did you tell them?"

"That you stayed here last night but left this morning on a motorbike. I thought that was safer than denying you'd been here, I'm a hopeless liar. One of them started swearing under his breath and the other gave me this poisonous smile. For a moment, I thought he was going to deck me."

Oberon frowned. "Do you think they believed you?"

"I think so," Ed replied. "But they didn't look happy about it. You need to be careful. Whoever they are, they're serious. I wouldn't want to run into either of them down a dark alley."

"Can you describe them?"

"One was thin, dark-eyed with bushy eyebrows," Ed replied. "The other one was bigger, always smiling and had a slight lisp. Both were English, from the accents. They're still out there, by their car."

Oberon ripped a blank sheet of paper from the notebook. He scribbled, "*Black Stone. Art had worked it out but couldn't act yet. I doubt if I can do any good now, especially as K is not decided about his plans. But if Mr. S. advises I will do the best I…*"

"What's that for?" Ed asked.

"Take this out to them and say you found it under the bed. Ask them to return it if they catch up with me."

Ed dashed away and a few minutes later Oberon heard the car start up then move away. He ventured downstairs to find Ed closing the door, his face flushed.

"I don't know what that bit of paper meant, but to say they weren't happy would be this year's understatement," he said. "They drove away so fast they'll probably crash around the next bend."

"We can only hope," Oberon muttered. "Later, I think you should drive to Fort William, to the police station. Describe the two men and say you suspect them of having had something to do with the London murder. You can say you overheard them talking. I'm pretty sure they'll come back. Not tonight, because we've sent them off on the wrong track, but first thing tomorrow morning. See if you can get the police to come here to meet them."

"I can do that. I actually have a friend working at the station in Fort William. I was at university with her. It was her who suggested this place to me."

"Even better. It'll be a good reason for you to call in in person rather than phoning."

"I'll head out straight away."

The round trip took Ed around three hours but he returned with good news.

"Angela will be here in the morning. She said the Met has several suspects for the murder, and they've an alert to look out for two men fitting the description I gave her."

"They're searching for *them*?"

"Yep. And for you. Angie had a picture of you."

"I didn't do it, honestly."

"I don't think you did, or I'd have brought Angela back here with me instead of a bag of Chinese food." Ed grinned. "I'll get it reheated, then we can eat, and you can tell me the real story."

Over chicken chow mein and prawn fried rice, Oberon told Ed everything. Ed's eyes got wider and wider as the story unfolded.

"So you see why I need to stay off the radar for a while longer."

"I'm glad I'm not in your shoes, that's for sure. Will you talk to Angela when she gets here in the morning?"

"I should because she might be able to help clear my name, but I can't. Not yet. I'll stay out of sight, see what goes down."

"It's your skin. I'm going to bed."

"Thank you, Ed. I mean it. I won't forget what you've done for me."

"No problem. I'll do what I can so long as I don't have to fight anyone. I bruise easily."

Oberon sat up until late, finishing the decoding of Art's notebook. He didn't realize how long he'd been there until the early dawn light seeped through the window shutters. With an aching back and stiff shoulders, he made his way upstairs but lay on the bed, fully dressed and wide awake. Every scenario he could think of played out in his head. There were so many things that could go wrong. He was banking on his enemies being predictable and that wasn't a safe bet. *I'll just have to hope that my luck holds.*

It was about six-thirty when he heard the sound of a car arriving. He crept across the landing to look out of a window where he could observe the approach road. *They must have been up early to get here so soon.* A redhead in a black suit and white blouse, who had to be Ed's friend Angela, accompanied by two uniformed PCs, got out of the car. After a brief conversation, one of the uniforms moved the car to the back of the house where it was out of sight then they all went inside. Oberon returned to his room and kept quiet until he heard the sound of a second car approaching. This one came from the opposite direction but didn't come up to the house, which meant he could see it from his window. It stopped about two hundred metres away in the shelter of a copse of trees then reversed carefully until it had all but disappeared from view. Oberon watched as two men approached until he lost sight of them around the corner of the house. It was tempting to creep down the stairs and attempt to listen in. Oberon would have loved to see the two men's reactions to coming face to face with the police. He hoped that bringing the police and his other, more dangerous, pursuers together, might work to his advantage. However, he couldn't risk it all going wrong and ending up in any of their hands.

"This plan is the dumbest thing you've ever come up with, Wycherley." He opened the window then dropped his pack into a bush. The drop was a bit further than he would have preferred but he swung a leg over the sill then swivelled around until he could hang by his fingertips. He kicked away from the wall before letting go. The landing was still jarring and once he retrieved his pack, he limped away, his knee throbbing. He crossed the lane, crawled down the bank of a stream then followed its course in the direction of the copse. A shambling run took him to the car, which was an older model BMW. He gave thanks that the car was old enough not to have an immobiliser but he needn't have worried because the key was in the ignition.

He gave a wry grin. "So they were after a quick getaway. Suckers." He stowed his pack on the back seat then got behind the wheel. Releasing the handbrake, he let the car roll as far as he could without starting the engine, then fired her up. He turned away from the cottage and as soon as he was out of sight, floored the accelerator, determined to gain as much distance as possible. "Sorry, Ed." He eyed the rear-view mirror. "I'll be back when it's safe for you to be near me. At least you have plenty of material for another book."

Chapter Five

The euphoria of escape didn't last long. Oberon drove far too fast over the narrow moorland roads, gaze constantly darting to the rear-view mirror. As he drove he thought about the information he'd deciphered in Art's notebook and his mind raced at the implications. Art's story hadn't quite been a pack of lies but it certainly hadn't been the whole truth. "I believed you, you little shit." Oberon thumped the steering wheel. "And it's all far worse than you said. You should have told me." Despite Art's deception, Oberon believed what he'd read in the book. *Why would anyone go to such lengths to conceal it if it isn't true?*

The fifteenth of June loomed ever closer and it was going to be a day that could change the course of the future, far surpassing the significance of the killing of one man, however influential. Kairos Doukas was a small part of a much bigger plan. *Perhaps Art was trying to protect me. He told me enough to get my attention but the truth is so dangerous no rational man would have agreed to be part of it. Art tried to shoulder the risk alone, the idiot. This is all far bigger than he could ever have dealt with without help.*

Most of the story was in the notes — though there were gaps, where the missing pieces would have been in Art's head. He'd documented the names of his sources, giving each of them a numerical value that seemed to relate to their reliability. One person, Debenham, got five out of a possible five and another, Boothe, got three. *It can't be a coincidence that both those names belong to members of the cabinet. Though of course they could be their family members.* An odd phrase appeared repeatedly in the notes, always within brackets. *("Thirty-nine steps").* The last time Art had written it, he'd elaborated – *("Thirty-nine steps, that's the place – high tide 10.17 p.m.").* "I solved the code and half of it's still gibberish," Oberon muttered. "Why couldn't you have been a bit more obvious, Art?"

Lacking a clear idea of where he should go next, Oberon headed east. The area was remote and there weren't many options for roads to take. Without a map or sat nav, Oberon followed his nose and the position of the sun. A gradual descent brought him off the moors and he travelled through meadows alongside a river. For miles, he drove alongside a boundary wall, catching glimpses of a castle through breaks in the trees. He passed ancient villages full of thatched cottages with gardens blazing with hawthorn and yellow laburnum. It was all so peaceful and sleepy that it was hard to believe that somewhere behind him were people who most likely wanted him dead.

In one hamlet he spotted a police car at the side of the road. He drove at one mile an hour under the speed limit, eyes fixed on the road, but his heart was pounding. He was sure he'd spot the car behind him and took several random turns until he thought it was safe to breathe easy again.

"Stealing a car was an idiot move," he scolded himself. "What were you thinking? You *weren't* thinking, that's the problem. Every cop from here to London could be looking for you and if they have a vehicle to track...fuck's sake." In his random driving, he'd managed to get turned around and began to recognise places he'd already passed. Taking smaller roads risked him getting stuck on a farm track or trapped at a dead end. If he abandoned the car and it was discovered, he wouldn't have enough of a head start to get away on foot.

The warning light on the fuel gauge turned red and Oberon cursed. In a few more miles, he wouldn't have any choice but to walk. He was also getting hungry and had little in the way of supplies in his pack. His hasty decision to run from Ed's cottage hadn't taken food into account. Distracted and anxious, he sped down a hill and failed to anticipate a sharp bend. He barely managed to control the car and slewed onto the straight. The blare of a horn sounded and he realized to his horror that another car was pulling out from between a pair of stone gate posts. He slammed on the brakes, but it was too late. He did the only thing he could to avoid hitting the other vehicle — he yanked the wheel hard to the left and swerved the BMW into the shrubbery on the side of the narrow road.

His hope for a soft, yielding landing was shattered as the car gave a sickening lurch then plunged forwards. The vehicle rocketed down a steep slope, and Oberon, acting on pure instinct with more than an edge of panic, forced the door open and hurled himself out.

He tumbled onto the ground, rolling over and over as the car continued its descent, crashing into a stream some forty metres below. The noise of smashing glass and bending metal was horrendous and an acrid smell of scorched rubber and spilt fuel filled the air.

Oberon's momentum was halted abruptly by a spiny thorn bush. Breathless, he lay there miserably trying to work out if he were dead or just wanted to be.

"Hey, are you hurt?" The shout came from the road above, from someone who sounded sympathetic but worried.

Fucking stupid question. "Minor damage only, I think," Oberon called back. Moving involved spikes doing their thing in sensitive places and wasn't fun.

"Hold on, I'm coming to you."

"Hold on to what exactly?"

"Funny. If you're attempting humour you can't be that badly hurt."

Oberon found himself looking up at a tall young woman wearing goggles and a leather flying jacket. "Are you wearing...goggles?"

"Haven't damaged your eyes then."

"No, I don't think so."

"I'm Francesca. Fran. I was about to leave for a vintage car meet at the Castle Arms." She scowled. "My MG has no roof. The goggles are practical." She held out a hand then hauled Oberon out of the bush. "You're bleeding."

"No shit. I landed in a dagger bush."

"It's gorse and it could have been worse. You could be down there with your car. I should call the police."

"No!" That was the last thing Oberon needed. "I mean, it was my fault. You're not hurt and your car is okay, right?"

"Yeah, but…"

"Look, I'll get a mate to come haul it out of the gully next week."

Fran seemed conflicted. "Okay, fine but I'll drop you back at my place so you can get fixed up. My brother arrived earlier and he can look after you while I get back to my noggin and natter."

"Your noggin and…never mind, I don't need to know. That would be kind. I believe there are thorns in my ass among other places I'd rather they weren't."

The pair of them scrambled up the slope to the road. Oberon hurt everywhere but didn't think anything was broken.

"Well the brat likes boys so I'm sure he won't charge to extract them." Fran grinned as she pushed back her goggles. "Your clothes are wrecked, did you have any luggage with you?"

"Just a rucksack, tent and stuff in the car. I was travelling light." He peered down the slope at the wreckage, the twisted metal of the BMW barely visible through the dense undergrowth. There was no way to retrieve anything from the car without ropes.

"Well, I'm not going down there now. The parental units are abroad but my dad's about your size. We'll find you something. Can't promise the latest fashion. Dad's more Barbour and Burberry than Paul Smith and Ralph Lauren."

"Clean and not ripped would be nice." Oberon eyed the tear in his trousers that exposed six inches of thigh.

Fran patted his shoulder. "Come on, I'll drive you up to the house."

"Nice car." Oberon admired the smart green MG parked on the verge. "What year?"

"1934. She's called Gertrude."

"Of course she is."

Fran adjusted her goggles. "Get in then. I haven't got all day."

She drove back through the stone pillars onto a narrow road that wound through the trees. Oberon, huddled low in his seat to avoid the wind, squinted at the passing scenery. "Where are we exactly?" To his astonishment, the castle he'd passed earlier in the day came into view, albeit from a different angle.

"Welcome to the family pile."

"Jesus. This place is huge."

"It's also drafty as hell and costs a fortune to maintain," Fran said, pulling up directly in front of an impressive carved door. Oberon levered himself out of the car with a groan and Fran ushered him to follow her inside. The arched reception hall they went into was dominated by a huge black marble fireplace and an impressive candelabra.

"Parts of it date back to the fourteenth century," Fran said. "Wait here a minute while I go dig the brat out of his cave."

She jogged up the stairs and Oberon did a full circle, taking in the family portraits and dark wood furniture. He was admiring a pair of enormous oriental vases when Fran returned, trailed by her brother.

Oberon gaped. "Syd?"

"Richard! When sis told me she'd brought in a battered stray, I had no idea it was you."

Fran shoved her brother. "You know him? How?"

"We met on the sleeper." Syd flushed.

"You mean you…Syd, you're such a slut! And you too…men!" Fran glared at both of them then spun on her heel. "I'm leaving you two to do whatever. You might want to find the first aid kit before you get up to anything energetic, Syd. He's a bit the worse for wear." There was a thud as she swung the huge door shut behind her.

"I thought you were in Fort William?" Oberon said, swaying on his feet.

"I was but when you called I left my grandma's place and came up here. I was going to try to track you down. I found the place you stayed, spoke to Ed and he said you'd moved on."

"How did you…?"

"You used the landline at his place, I called the number back. But that doesn't matter. Fran said you crashed your car."

"Yeah, avoiding her. She came out of your gates like she was competing in a cross country rally."

"She drives like a lunatic. You're hurt. Can you make it upstairs? You can take a shower and I'll inspect the damage."

"Yeah. I managed to get out of the car before it got airborne but landed in a gorse bush. Could have been softer."

"You're lucky you didn't break your neck. Come on."

Oberon followed Syd to a spacious bathroom with a claw-foot tub and separate shower. It was on a corner of the building and boasted two enormous windows.

"If you sit on the toilet, you can admire the mountains," Syd said. "Take your clothes off."

Oberon blinked, his vision blurring. "I think I might have hit my head a bit…"

"Fuck." Syd guided him to the toilet then pushed him down onto it. "Put your head between your knees. I'll run a bath. It'll be easier for you than standing in the shower and I'll be here to make sure you don't drown."

"That would be good. You could get in with me, that thing's big enough to swim in."

"Oh, not totally out of it then?"

"I have a hard skull." Oberon managed to strip off his fleece and T-shirt but struggled with his trousers until Syd helped with the button and zipper. "Thanks." He didn't trust himself to stand so he wriggled out of them, but they got stuck around his ankles.

Syd started running the bath, then dropped to his knees to unlace Oberon's boots.

"That's a good spot for you," Oberon said with a weak smile.

"Thought you'd like it. You're slurring a bit. You might have a concussion and...wow, that's quite the collection of cuts and bruises." Syd pulled a thorn out of Oberon's thigh.

"Ow."

"There are plenty more where that one came from."

"Wonderful." Oberon got out of the rest of his clothes.

"How about you lie on the floor and I'll fetch some tweezers?"

For the next fifteen minutes, Oberon lay prone on a pile of towels, head resting on his folded arms, while Syd extracted thorns from his skin.

"How did you get so many in your backside? Not that I'm complaining—the view is great."

Oberon groaned. "I'm so pleased you're having a good time. You're never going to let me forget this are you?"

"Absolutely not. Right, I think that's all of them. Haul yourself into the tub. You're too big for me to lift."

"Thank God."

The hot water, scented with something herbal, felt amazing and his cuts and scratches only stung for a minute or two.

"You really have got yourself into a state, haven't you?" Syd perched on the side of the bath, swirling a finger through the water.

"I've been worse."

"That's not a good thing!"

"Fell down a mine shaft once. Rusty ladder rung gave way under me. Broke my ankle but still had to climb out — there wasn't any other way."

"Fuck!"

"Yeah. Got fanged by a grumpy snake in the Amazon. Knifed by even grumpier bandits in Colombia. The scar on my back is from an iron rail that I fell on during an earthquake in New Zealand."

"How are you still alive?"

"I heal quickly."

"How's your head? Do you feel sick?"

"Aching and no. A decent night's sleep and I'll be fine. I don't want to impose though."

"This place has eleven bedrooms, Obi. You could stay here a month and no one would notice. Fran has a place in Inverness. She's only here housesitting because the 'rents are swanning around the south of France on holiday."

"Shouldn't that be castle sitting?"

Syd grabbed a washcloth and threw it at Oberon. "Get clean. I'll find you some of dad's pyjamas to wear — don't worry, he always gets them for Christmas but never wears them, so they'll be like new."

"Did you just tell me your dad sleeps in the nude?"

"If it helps, so do I. Must be a family trait." Syd left the room before Oberon could comment. He stared at the door Syd had left through.

"Really? He's leaving me with that?" He did his best to clean up and as far as he could tell none of the scratches were deep. Leaving the hot water was a wrench but the fluffy towel he grabbed was warm. He made sure to pat rather than rub himself dry. Syd soon returned with a pair of tartan flannel pyjamas.

"Here you go. They're tartan so you'll fit right in."

"Thanks. I think."

"Ingrate. You hungry?"

"Starving."

Syd lobbed a balled-up pair of thick socks at him. "Here. The kitchen has flagstones so you'll need them. I brought you an old pullover to wear, too. It might be early summer but this place could freeze the balls off a polar bear."

"Nice image, thanks." Oberon dropped his towel and Syd licked his lips. "You know you're ogling an accident victim, right?"

"Ooh, yeah."

"Shameless."

"I thought you knew that already."

Once he was dressed, Oberon followed Syd to the kitchen where he heated up some soup. They sat at the kitchen table and Oberon ate while Syd watched him.

"What?" Oberon scraped out the bowl.

"You want to tell me what's going on? Why were you in a car at all? Why was Ed so cagey about you when I spoke to him? And what's this?" Syd put Art's notebook on the table. "It was in your fleece pocket."

Oberon sighed. "You don't want to know."

"Yes I do. I fed you soup, *and* I pulled thorns out of your rear, so you owe me."

"You're not going to let this go, are you?"

"Not a chance."

"I don't want to put you in danger. Sometimes, too much knowledge is a bad thing, Syd."

"How about we start with something simple. Is Richard your real name?"

"No, sorry."

"I knew it! So…"

"Fine! My name is Oberon Wycherley." It was a relief to tell the truth.

"You have to be kidding me? Nobody is called Oberon."

Oberon stared at Syd.

"Really?"

"Really."

"Were your parents high?"

"Probably. Dad was into amateur dramatics. Mom did his costume for *A Midsummer Night's Dream*. The rest is history."

"So do people call you Ron?"

"Absolutely not."

"Ronnie?"

"Obi."

"Okay, you've started. That didn't hurt a bit, did it? Now tell me the rest." Syd settled back in his chair.

Oberon recognized the moment his resolve wavered. He gazed around the room, looking for inspiration from the old prints on the walls or the family photos stuck to the fridge door. *It's all so normal.* "All right. That notebook is the key to something big. Bigger than I realized at first. There's a plan set in motion for the fifteenth of June that could change everything. I was in that car because I was running for my life. Ed's cagey because he knows how dangerous this is."

"You're not making much sense."

"Sorry." Oberon started again and gave Syd the full story from meeting Art and discovering his murder through to the escape from London, the coded notebook and his theories about who was after him. At some point, Syd got up and began pacing the length of the kitchen.

"So, first things first — you're sure there's no way to prevent this Doukas dude from coming to the UK?"

"I suppose there could be, but Art suggested that would be worse than Doukas being here. He's an important part of the equation."

"Okay, so second, whatever happens when he's here will set off a series of events that will benefit some very nasty people."

"Apparently. From what I've pieced together, if our philanthropic Greek fails to announce his plans for a greener world, it'll be spun as a reason to discredit all the science that proves the dangers of global warming, deforestation, fossil fuels… Governments desperate for investment will seize the opportunity to authorize, even encourage, environmentally damaging exploration and projects instead."

"That could be impossible to reverse."

"There's more. Doukas's death will be falsely linked to Muslim interests in the Middle East, setting off oil wars. The Americans will likely issue an ultimatum, which Russia won't take lying down. The European Union will attempt to play the peacemaker, and pour oil on the waters. Tensions will escalate."

"This could lead to war." Syd's face was pale.

"And countries at war are far less likely to take notice, or care about, the environmental rape going on right under their noses if it's putting money in their war chests." Oberon frowned. "It sounds so far-fetched, but Art discovered that something else is due to happen on June fifteenth. Something that will look like a terrorist attack."

"Fuck. What kind of attack? What's the target?

"From Art's notes, he believed that all of this is being orchestrated by a group calling themselves the Black Stone. He wasn't specific about what the main event is going to be."

"I'm amazed these people ever let you get out of London," Syd said.

"I've thought about that. I can only assume that they didn't want to draw attention to themselves in such a public place. I was easy to set up as responsible for Art's murder. I thought I was being clever coming up here, but I might have been incredibly stupid. Who would question it if I met with an unfortunate accident hiking alone in wild country?"

"You're not a secret agent. I'd say you've done okay so far."

"Remains to be seen. But you realise," Oberon concluded, "you're sheltering a murder suspect. I'm a wanted man. My mugshot is probably on posters in police station break rooms up and down the country. You should call the police and have me arrested. I'm not in much condition to run."

"I don't think you'd get very far *with* the police," Syd mused. "From the sounds of it, they wouldn't offer much protection from the people who are after you. If this Black Stone group has as much influence as Art thought, there might be members *in* the force."

"Even so, it would be safer for you to hand me over."

"I don't think so and besides, you've grown on me." Syd gave him a lopsided grin. "Did you really travel all over as a mining engineer?"

Oberon nodded. "Yes. Meeting Art was pure accident. He was renting a flat in my building and singled me out to help him."

"That's a dangerous profession, isn't it? You must know how to look after yourself."

"I guess. I've been in some interesting situations. More than I told you about in the bathroom."

"I'll just bet you have." Syd laughed. "You're no murderer. You also have excellent taste in men, so I'm in. What can I do to help?"

Relief washed over him and Oberon sagged with fatigue. "Not very exciting, I know, but do you think you could point me to a bed? Maybe after a night's rest we'll be able to come up with a plan together but for now, I'm barely functioning."

Syd held out his hand and Oberon took it. He let Syd tow him through the castle then up a spiral stone staircase to a turret room.

"My bedroom," Syd said. "I think the idea was that I could make as much noise as I wanted up here as a kid and no one would care."

At some point, the room had been updated from teenage décor to something more sophisticated because there weren't many signs of Syd's childhood. A king-size bed, covered in a dark-coloured patchwork quilt, dominated the space. It was complemented by solid oak furniture that must have been a nightmare to haul up the stairs. The room wasn't completely round because a small section had been walled off to house a sink and toilet.

"Do you mind? Sleeping with me, I mean," Syd asked.

"As long as you're not expecting anything more than unconsciousness," Oberon replied with a touch of regret.

"I think I can resist your charms for one night, Kenobi."

"You did *not* just call me that."

"I did. It's a miracle I resisted this long, in fact." Syd pulled back the covers. "Get in."

"If I wasn't so fucking tired, I'd spank your behind until it glowed pink."

"Another time, when I can't outrun you."

Oberon took off his borrowed jumper then got into the bed. "Oh, this is so comfortable."

"New mattress." Syd stripped, letting his clothes drop where he stood, then scrambled into bed next to Oberon. He pressed close against him. "I shouldn't have given you pyjamas. Want skin on skin." He kissed Oberon's neck. "Please?"

With a bit of wriggling, and stoic ignoring of pain, Oberon discarded the tartan flannel. "Better?" It felt nice to have Syd's smooth body in contact with his.

"Definitely. I promise not to molest you while you sleep. Much."

Oberon grunted. "Don't think I'll notice." He was halfway to sleep already. *A castle turret has to be safe, right?* He pulled Syd even closer then drifted away.

Chapter Six

When Oberon awoke, Syd was gone, and his side of the bed was cool. Oberon lay there for a while with his eyes shut, mulling over the last few days. None of what had happened to him had been in his imagination. *The only good thing to come out of this whole fucked-up mess is Syd and in the light of a new day, he's probably going to throw me out on my ear. Either that or there'll be cops in the kitchen enjoying a pre-arrest bacon sandwich.*

Oberon hauled himself out of bed and went to find the bathroom. He took a quick shower then dried off. There was no sign of Syd but when Oberon got back to the turret room, a pile of clean clothes had appeared on the bed. The worn jeans were a good fit. There was a heather-coloured wool pullover and a checked shirt, both excellent quality. Socks and underwear were still new in their packages. Oberon's boots had been cleaned but he padded down the stairs in his socks. He didn't want to give Syd the impression he was leaving.

He found Syd in the kitchen with his sister. Fran was sitting at the table cradling a mug of coffee and nibbling on a slice of charred toast. Syd was frying bacon in a huge skillet on the stove.

"He scrubs up well, brat. Not bad. My jeans look great on him." Fran raised her mug to Oberon. "Any chance you swing both ways?"

"Hey!" Syd whacked her with a spatula. "Hands off, he's mine. Go find one of your own."

Fran pouted. "Around here?"

"Farmers are desperate men. You'd be in with a chance when there's nothing but sheep and Highland cattle for miles. Although sheep don't talk back so…"

"Cheeky little shit. I should smack you but I don't have the energy."

"I apologise for my sister, Obi. She's hungover and has no filter."

"And you do?" Fran retorted. "Sit down, Obi, there's probably a burnt offering coming your way."

Oberon eyed her toast. "Yeah?"

Syd plonked a plate of bacon, eggs and golden toast in front of him. "Eat up."

"How come his doesn't look like it spent two hours in a furnace?" Fran complained. "Mine's been cremated." She stole a piece of Obi's toast.

"Because he's my favourite and quit complaining, or you can make your own." Syd sat next to Oberon with his own plate. "I was going to let you sleep in."

"Thanks, but I don't think I should stay here too long, do you?"

"Fran knows everything, you can talk in front of her."

Fran shrugged. "We have a secret passage if you need to use it." She sneaked a rasher of bacon.

"That might come in useful because the longer I'm here, the more likely it is that these Black Stone people will find me," Oberon said. "They've been using a drone. They may have spotted the car by now."

"Not likely, Fran hauled it into the barn with the 4X4 before first light." Syd chomped on a mushroom. "Your bag was intact. It's in the hall. We have time to make a plan."

"Thanks, Fran. We?"

"Well, you've not done the best job on your own, so far, have you?"

"This isn't exactly my sphere of expertise, you know."

"Which is precisely why you need the assistance of someone with superior intellect and general sneakiness."

Fran chuckled. "I know what you're thinking, Obi, and yes, a spanking would do him the world of good. Trouble is he'd probably enjoy it too much."

Oberon shook his head but couldn't hide a smile. "Tell me about it."

"I'm right here!" Syd exclaimed.

"Like we could forget," Fran snarked. "I've been trying for years."

"Well, we have to decide what to do next," Oberon said. "Staying under the radar is nigh on impossible in this day and age, even here."

"Technology sucks. Not all technology, obviously, because I'm kind of fond of the internet and all its deliciousness, but in this particular situation. It is sucky. Getting to the point...let's say we've bought ourselves twenty-four hours," Syd said. "There are *some* advantages to being landed gentry. Connections. The old boy network is a powerful thing."

"Syd, who exactly is your dad?" Oberon asked.

"Uh, he's the Earl of Whatten."

"So that makes you a…"

"Viscount."

"Fuck."

"Apparently you've already been there, done that," Fran muttered with a smirk. "I don't suppose he's told you his full name is Sydenham, either?"

"Sis, really?" Syd threw a mushroom at her. "You'd never guess *she* was a Lady, would you?"

Oberon stared at the bickering siblings.

"Do you have an obnoxious younger brother, Obi?" Fran asked.

"I'm an only child. Fuck, your father is going to hang me off the battlements by my balls when he finds out what I've dragged the two of you into."

"What he doesn't know won't hurt him," Syd said. "But seriously, we do have connections with some useful people. People I know we can trust."

"So what do we do? We can't trust electronic communication."

"Snail mail. We'll put good old-fashioned pen to paper and post a letter. First class from here will take a couple of days to arrive, but there's time."

"Are you sure about trusting them though? Art said there are some very important people involved in this."

"Obi, the Head of MI5 is my godfather. I'm ninety-nine point nine per cent sure he's not a bad guy."

"Why am I not fucking surprised?"

Syd shrugged. "I'm a man of many secrets. Disclaimers though, about the nought point five percent. He's that much bad because he once sent me to my room without supper."

Fran gave an exasperated sigh. "You fell in the lake, Obi, when you'd been specifically told not to go near the water."

"I saw fishes. It was justified."

"You were in your smart clothes for a christening. You made everyone late."

"There was sticky toffee pudding for afters that night. The punishment was way too extreme."

"Christ on a stick." Oberon groaned. "Perhaps it would be better if I go to see him in person. You could write a letter of introduction, convince him I'm worth seeing."

Syd smacked his sister. "That could work. He has a second home in the Lake District. He'll be there in a few days' time because he's a creature of habit and always goes at this time of year. I can let him know we're in the area and will be dropping in for a visit."

"We? There is no 'we' here, Syd," Oberon said. "You'll be in enough trouble as it is, letting me hide here."

"There is no I in team, mister. Of course there is a 'me' if you play with the letters but let's ignore that. It'll be much easier to get to see Uncle Mo if I'm with you."

"He has a point," Fran said. "For once. I can't believe I'm siding with him."

Oberon frowned. "It would mean leaving you here on your own, Fran. What if people from Black Stone show up here?"

Syd laughed. "Then they'll be in a whole world of pain."

"I'd really like them to call." Fran cracked her knuckles. "I've been meaning to get in some crossbow practice."

"She's not kidding, is she?" Oberon asked Syd.

"Nope." Syd poured more coffee. "You see what I had to put up with when I was a kid?"

"You made it to your twenties alive, what's the problem?" Fran glared.

"That was more luck than anything." Syd stacked their plates then took them across to the sink. "Why don't we have a dishwasher?" He ran the water with a sigh. "This is so last century."

"If the police come here, Fran, tell them about the car wreck," Oberon said. "You didn't know who I was so you helped me out with a lift to the nearest rail station, then say I caught a train south but didn't mention where I was going." Oberon drummed his fingers on the table, thinking. "Say you pulled the car out of the stream because it was a hazard to wildlife or something. I don't want them thinking you were harbouring a fugitive."

Fran sucked down more coffee. "I dated the local police inspector. Believe me, he won't be a problem. Now, I have hungry chickens to feed. When do you think you'll leave?"

"After dark," Oberon said. "Less chance of being spotted from above."

Syd, who was up to his elbows in soapy water, glanced over his shoulder. "We'll head to the lodge for a couple of days, Fran. Hole up out of sight before we head south. I don't want to beat the letter to Uncle Mo and the whole idea of Obi being up here was to kill some time."

"The lodge?" Oberon asked.

"We have a hunting lodge in the mountains. It dates back to when there used to be grouse hunting parties. We keep it as a family bolt hole for weekends away. It's a good base for hiking and for hiding out. There's only one road in—it's pretty isolated."

"There's only one bed…" Fran cast a sly glance their way as she got to her feet.

"I'm sure we'll cope." Syd stuck his tongue out at her. "Go find a chicken to torment."

"I'll have you know my girls are pampered queens, which is why your breakfast eggs keep coming."

She gave him the finger then blew a kiss to Oberon. "Later. Be good."

Once Fran had gone, Syd found notepaper and envelopes in a drawer. He scribbled a quick, innocuous note to his godfather and, before sealing the envelope, slipped a dried forget-me-not flower from a little plastic packet between the folds of the paper. "So he knows it's genuinely from me."

"You have secret correspondence codes in your family?" Oberon asked, intrigued.

"It's just a silly thing we started when I was a kid. My parents were trying to encourage me to read and write more when all I wanted to do was climb trees and take my bike out. They roped in Uncle Mo—he's not really my uncle but we always called him that—and he devised spy games to get me interested. The flower was something he dreamt up and considering the current circumstances, it's a useful precaution. It'll also let him know that this is a serious situation."

"So Mo is short for…"

"Morris. Sir Morris Stanley, to be precise."

"I can't believe how lucky I was to meet you on the train, Syd. Not sure what I'd be doing now if it wasn't for your connections."

"The Fates were at work that day, weren't they? You'd be doing fine, though the odds are stacked against you. One man against this organisation, whoever they are, is not a fair contest."

"Yeah. I wouldn't recommend placing a bet on my chances. Do you have a map? I'd like to get a look at where we're going."

"Sure. I think there's an old OS map in my room. We need to stay off all electronics from now on. Leave no trace of our plans."

"This situation brings home how much we rely on the internet for everything now, doesn't it?"

"It does. In fact, I can leave my phone here and get Fran to use it to make it seem like I'm still around. It's only a matter of time before I'm connected with you, if it hasn't already happened."

"That's a good idea. I only have the cheap burner phone I bought in London but I can leave that here too. Have you done this sort of thing before?"

"Aided and abetted a wanted man? Not recently." Syd grinned. "I knew you'd make an interesting friend."

"So you didn't fuck me for a comfortable night on the train then?"

"Well..."

"Syd..."

"Those recliners are uncomfortable, okay?" He chuckled. "No! I let you fuck me because you're gorgeous. You have an intriguing face." Syd reached out and traced Oberon's cheek with a finger. "I'd like to keep seeing it—and other bits, of course."

"Yeah? Not sick of me yet?"

Syd blushed. "Shall we go find that map? There are some unusual...contours I'd like to show you." He peeked from beneath his lashes.

"I'm always up for in-depth exploration of the local landmarks," Oberon said as he pushed his chair back.

Syd was scrambling out of his clothes from the moment they entered his turret room. Oberon watched him and once he was fully naked pushed him against the wall. He took a firm hold of Syd's cock then sucked up a mark on his neck.

"What would you say if I told you I want you over my knee?"

"What do you want me to say?" Syd's voice shook and he pressed closer to Oberon.

"How about *yes please, Sir*?" Oberon squeezed Syd's straining cock a bit harder.

"Oh God! Yes!" Syd squirmed and moaned. "Please, Sir."

"Very good. It's about time I reminded your cheeky ass who's in charge." Oberon held Syd in place a while longer, staring into his eyes, trying to judge Syd's willingness. Syd's gaze burned with intensity.

"You're sure you want this?"

"I'm sure. I *am*. Feel." Syd held Oberon's palm to his chest. "Feel how hard my heart is pounding."

Oberon pulled Syd over to the bed. Syd didn't resist but whimpered softly as Oberon sat on the edge of the mattress and got comfortable. He patted his thighs. "Up you come."

After a failed first attempt and a lot of giggling, Syd managed to lie across Oberon's lap with his arms dangling and bum in the air.

"Comfortable?" Oberon asked, shifted his thighs to give Syd more stability. He made sure Syd's cock was lodged between his legs.

"Not really, but that's not what this is about, is it?"

"Have you ever been spanked before?"

"No but I've dreamt about it. A lot."

"Feeling vulnerable?" Oberon stroked Syd's bare behind.

"Yes." The word came out as a squeak.

"Safe word is red for now. If you need to, use it. I mean it, Syd. No false bravado. If you're not having a good time, this stops."

Syd let out a shaky sigh. "Okay."

His safe word wasn't forthcoming so Oberon wasted no time. He spanked Syd's firm round buttocks with his open palm, gradually increasing the weight of his blows. Syd jerked and moaned but sounded like he was enjoying himself. From the rough sting in his palm, Oberon could imagine the burning sensation Syd must be experiencing. He paused.

"You want more?"

"Don't stop! Sooo good."

"Not sure that's the idea, Syd." As each swat landed, Syd writhed, his hips bucking. "I could get addicted to this." Oberon was breathing as heavily as Syd. The more Oberon spanked, the more his own body betrayed him. His cock was rock hard, throbbing, and the sight of Syd's vulnerable backside turning pink only fuelled his arousal.

Syd's moans grew louder and more desperate. He seemed lost in pleasure, pushing his backside towards Oberon's blows. Oberon stopped spanking and reached beneath Syd's body to grasp his cock. He stroked it firmly, drawing out every drop of intensity he could. Syd cried out, his body convulsing as he came.

Finally, as Syd's orgasm subsided, he relaxed, his body limp. Oberon lifted him to his feet, pulling him close. "There," Oberon whispered, "was that worth waiting for?"

Syd nodded weakly, still catching his breath. He met Oberon's gaze, his eyes bright. "That was fucking amazing."

Oberon led Syd to the tiny bathroom, guiding him to sit on the toilet. He ran warm water into the sink and soaked a washcloth. Syd had a quick wipe down and when he was done, Oberon wrapped him in a towel.

"You want to go for a shower?"

"I feel all woozy. I don't want to walk to the bathroom now."

"Not surprising. How about putting some clothes on?"

"I'd much rather you fucked me." Syd pressed a hand against Oberon's bulging crotch.

"Oh you would, would you?"

"Definitely. I'm still horny and it's all your fault. I think you have an obligation to follow through." He dropped the towel.

Oberon let his gaze linger on the way Syd's muscles flexed beneath his skin as he moved. It was an indulgence, but Syd's lithe body was worthy of admiration.

"You're beautiful."

"Why, thank you." Syd preened. He took Oberon's hand and pulled him into the bedroom. "Kiss me."

"I'm the one giving the orders, remember?" Oberon put a finger beneath Syd's chin and tilted his head back.

"Whatever you say." Syd puckered his lips. "Want smooches."

Oberon didn't argue but captured Syd's lips in a demanding kiss. Syd gave as good as he got, wrapping his arms around Oberon so he couldn't get away.

Oberon's cock wanted more. He lifted Syd onto the bed where he spread out, his expression expectant.

"What are you waiting for?"

Oberon shed his clothes. Not much daylight penetrated the room from the narrow window and Syd turned on a bedside lamp for an added glow.

"That mouth of yours will get you into trouble."

"Goody."

Oberon crawled onto the bed and held himself over Syd, clear air between them. He kissed Syd's neck, savouring the salt on his skin as he traced a path to his collarbone. Syd reached for him, pulling him close until they touched from hip to chest.

"Making love in the daytime feels decadent, doesn't it?" Syd murmured.

"It does." Oberon kissed his shoulder. "You've taken your punishment, now comes pleasure." He brushed Syd's lips with his own before deepening the kiss.

When he pulled away, Syd took a ragged breath. "Fuck, Obi. The anticipation is killing me. Need you in me."

Oberon brushed a fingertip over Syd's lips. "Impatient." He flipped them over so that Syd was on top. "Ride me." Syd let out a soft moan as Oberon took hold of his cock. "Hard again. I'm impressed."

"Take it as a compliment." Syd groped for a condom, slipped it onto Oberon's straining dick then reached for the lube on the bedside table. He applied it quickly and Oberon squirmed.

"It's cold!"

"Wuss." Syd thrust two well-lubed fingers into his channel, prepping himself. Oberon gaped, transfixed, as Syd writhed, his lips parted. "You ready for me?"

"Less talking, more action, Syd."

Syd got into position, straddling Oberon's hips on his knees, then lowered himself onto Oberon's cock. He grunted. "Forgot how big you are."

"Take it slow."

"Wow, so full."

Oberon's eyes fluttered shut as the warmth of Syd's body surrounded him. "Feels good."

"You can watch, you know."

Oberon glared. "Careful, brat. I'm sure I can rustle up a blindfold for you."

Syd rose and fell, his abs rippling. He pinched his lower lip between his teeth and tilted his head back, exposing the lines of his throat. Pure ecstasy was etched on his features. Oberon grabbed his hips and helped him ride faster, jerking his hips to get deeper into Syd's body.

"Can't stop it," Syd moaned through gritted teeth. With a hard thrust, Oberon growled as the intense pleasure of release washed over him. Syd met his gaze as he too reached his climax, his body convulsing as his cum splattered Oberon's belly.

For a while, Syd sat, impaled, breathing heavily. Eventually, he lifted himself free then flopped onto the bed. Oberon went to the bathroom to deal with the condom. When he returned, he thought Syd might have dropped off to sleep but his eyes flickered open and a lazy smile spread across his face.

"That was so good."

Oberon lay next to him, his skin still flushed and warm. "It's a shame we have to get back to reality."

"Another five minutes won't hurt." Syd squirmed close and Oberon drew him into a cuddle.

"You're far too big of a distraction to be safe."

"I like the idea of being a bit dangerous."

"I'm beginning to regret longing for adventure. There's a lot to be said for a quiet, predictable life," Oberon said.

"You're only saying that because you're not in control of what's happening and I don't think you're used to that, are you?" Syd responded. "If you could control your destiny you'd revel in the excitement. Your career, your travels...not many men choose such a dangerous path. There's an adrenaline junkie under that cool exterior."

"Hmm, maybe once." Oberon thought about it as they dozed. Syd was a good judge of character, apparently, and insightful, considering he hadn't known Oberon very long.

Once they'd both regained some energy, Syd fetched a map. He spread it out on the bed then sat cross-legged next to it. He pointed out the main rail line to the south, which helped Oberon work out the lay of the land.

"The lodge is in quite wild country north of here." Syd tapped the location of the castle then traced a line into the mountains.

Oberon threw a pillow into Syd's lap. "Stop tempting me."

Syd snorted. "Been there, done that. Definitely going to get the T-shirt."

"One spanking not enough for you?"

"Not nearly."

Oberon shook his head. "You're a fucking handful. How long will it take us to get to the lodge?"

"If we leave after dark and drive without lights, we can do it in under two hours, I'd guess. It's not that far as the crow flies, but the roads are bad and you don't need another crash in your life just yet."

"Okay. We have a plan then." Oberon was glad to have something to think about and plan for. He needed to be doing something, not waiting around for things to happen *to* him. "Let's hope we can stay one step ahead of the enemy."

Chapter Seven

After a slow, somewhat hair-raising drive through the darkness, Oberon and Syd arrived at the Whatten Lodge in the early hours of the morning. They hadn't passed a single other vehicle on the way. Syd parked his car, a battered, lime green Mini, under a low shelter at the back of the building. Oberon pried his stiff fingers from the handle he'd been gripping. He stretched his hand and rotated his wrist.

"My driving is not *that* bad," Syd protested.

"If I were a cat," Oberon said, "I'd be down to three lives and the rest would be on life support."

"I know I was going a tad fast when we took off over that humpback bridge, but I'm sure you got used to worse road conditions abroad."

"Road conditions yes, driving no."

"I got us here, didn't I?" Syd pouted.

"You did and I'm grateful I didn't have to drive," Oberon admitted. "We're here and I'm looking forward to getting my head on a pillow."

They got out of the car and collected their overnight bags from the boot.

"This is a bit more upscale than I was expecting," Oberon said as they approached the substantial, red-brick building. "I pictured something a lot more rustic."

"Let me do my real estate pitch," Syd said. "The property boasts a double bedroom, a bathroom, with a shower and a bath and a cosy sitting room." He opened the front door with a flourish. "Which has an open log fire and there's an oil Rayburn in the kitchen along with a gas fridge freezer. The water is heated by the Rayburn and as well as an assortment of lamps and candles, additional light is powered by a couple of solar panels Dad had installed."

"I'm sold. It's really cosy."

"It's basic but fun. It was always an adventure coming up here when we were kids. Mum has filled it over the years with an assortment of random paraphernalia, which you can view in the morning, but we should get some rest now."

Oberon was stiff and sore after the drive. Previously invisible bruises from the crash were blooming on his skin. "I can't wait. Bed sounds good."

"You're a bit grey around the gills. Go on up and settle in. I'll get the heating sorted because this place gets cold even at this time of year. Top of the stairs, door on the right. The bathroom is to the left. The bed should be made up."

Oberon didn't argue. He found the bedroom, dropped off his bag then made use of the bathroom. The cold water made it a quick visit. Once he was done, he wandered back to the bedroom. Clanking from below told him Syd was still dealing with the Raeburn so he stripped off then climbed into what proved to be a very comfortable bed. He stretched out, determined to stay awake until Syd joined him, but his eyelids drooped and that was the last he knew until morning.

When Oberon awoke the next day, Syd was sleeping soundly next to him. Oberon watched him for a while, wondering at how innocent he seemed with the early morning light playing across his face. *What have I done, pulling him into this mess? I should have left him back at the castle.* A pang of guilt and the call of his bladder got him out of bed. He pulled on jeans and a jumper then padded across the landing to the bathroom. Urgent needs met, he made his way downstairs to the kitchen where he thanked working in remote places for his knowledge of oil-fired ranges. It didn't take long for him to produce a pot of coffee and, mug in hand, he shoved his feet in his shoes before venturing outside.

It was cool and fresh with only a light breeze. Behind the lodge, a rough track climbed through a long cleft in the hills. Syd had said it only went to an abandoned croft. To the front of the building, beyond a small piece of hard-standing, was a flat area, pitted with bog-holes and rough marshland. The glint of water between tussocks gave away how wet it was. Further off, heather-clad mountains were wreathed in blue mist. Other than the occasional bird call, it was blissfully quiet.

Oberon sipped his coffee and breathed deeply. It was a beautiful spot but the ambience was ruined when, half an hour later, he heard an ominous beat in the air.

"Fuck." He didn't dare move in case it drew attention.

A helicopter was coming up from the east. It was flying high, but as he looked it dropped several hundred feet and began to circle round a mountain peak in narrowing loops, just as a hawk wheels before it attacks. It got lower and Oberon caught a flash of light off glass as if someone in the cockpit was using binoculars. "Double fuck." There was no way they could fail to spot him and he wasn't wearing a hat. His hair was a giveaway if they were looking for him.

Suddenly, the helicopter began to rise in swift whorls, and the next he knew it was speeding eastward again until it became a dark speck against the morning sky.

"Was that a helicopter?"

Oberon jumped. He hadn't heard Syd come up behind him. "Christ, Syd, you almost gave me a heart attack and yes, it was."

"Looking for you?"

"They were searching for something, so probably."

"Did they spot you?" Syd peered into the distance.

"Can't be sure but I'd guess so. I shouldn't have come out here. There was nowhere to hide."

"You couldn't know they'd make such an early start. They'll have to land then find their way back here. This isn't an easy place to find if you don't know where you're going. We have some time."

"To go where? They could throw a cordon around this place with sufficient men. We can't drive out, there's only one road."

"Always with the negativity. Trust me."

Oberon gave Syd a better look. He was adorably tousled, wearing pyjama bottoms and an old sweater. He'd put on a pair of yellow wellies. Oberon grinned. "Cute footwear."

"Fuck off. Is there more coffee?"

"Pot's on the range."

"That might make up for you not being in bed with me when I woke up." Syd ambled back inside, rubbing at his eyes. Oberon followed, a bit perturbed at Syd's lack of urgency.

Syd downed an entire mug of coffee and poured another before he spoke. "We let them come."

"That's your plan? Why would we do that?"

"Because we need them looking elsewhere for a day or two and this gives us an opportunity to make sure that happens. It won't be difficult. There's no point in running because that moves the problem down the road and they have the resources to stay on our tails."

"So we let them walk in here?"

"Yes, but they're only going to find me, getting this place ready for a family break."

"And where will I be?"

"Not far away, I'll show you in a bit. When I'm fully conscious."

"What about my hair? They must have seen it."

"I have a white woolly hat I can put on. From the distance they were at they wouldn't be able to tell the difference."

"I don't like the idea of leaving you here alone."

"Mr. Over Protective. I'll be fine. Remember, they're the ones looking for a needle in a haystack and besides, I don't think we have a lot of choice, do you?"

"I was stupid. I should have thought about what I was doing."

"No, you weren't. If they've linked us together, they'd have found this place eventually. Now we have a bit of time to prepare. We should eat. I can do porridge with UHT milk. That'll have to do because the fridge is empty."

After breakfast, they spent some time making sure that the lodge seemed occupied by one person rather than two, which wasn't difficult as they'd hardly settled in. Syd got Oberon to dress in warm dark clothes then they hiked a short way from the building, Oberon shouldering his pack.

Syd guided him towards a rocky outcrop. He skirted some huge granite boulders then disappeared into some undergrowth.

"Where the heck has he gone?" Oberon almost fell into the hole at his feet but Syd grabbed his ankle from below.

"Careful."

"What the hell?" Oberon sat on the edge of the hole then shimmied underground. He dropped about a foot into a short, damp crawl space, moved through it on his hands and knees then was able to stand. Syd had brought a solar lantern with him, which gave out enough light to reveal a cave, just big enough for Oberon to stretch his arms out.

"What is this place?"

Syd shrugged. "Fran and I found it when we were kids. Fell into it, in fact. It's a natural cave but was probably used by the Jacobites. We found a buckle in here and some musket balls. They're back at the lodge somewhere. It can't be seen from above and unless you know where it is, it's very hard to find. No–one is going to stumble over it by accident."

"It was you who fell down the hole, wasn't it?" Oberon said, grinning.

"Of course it was. I sprained an ankle. Fran had zero sympathy, needless to say." He moved closer. "Kiss me. I want the taste of you on my lips."

Oberon leaned in, capturing Syd's lips in a hungry kiss. As they broke apart, their eyes locked in silent understanding.

"Be safe, Syd. I won't be happy if you get hurt."

Syd reached for Oberon's hand, intertwining their fingers. "I'll be fine, I'm a good liar."

"I hope so." Oberon traced the cold stone with his fingers. "Good thing I'm not claustrophobic."

"With your career? Hardly. The walls seem to whisper in here, don't they? I like to imagine rebels seeking refuge and lovers finding solace in the shadows."

"You're a romantic."

"Maybe. I *am* thinking about introducing you to the rug in front of the open fire later. Crackling flames, bare skin, your dick in my ass..."

"Christ, Syd. Get rid of them quickly, for fuck's sake." Oberon's cock twitched. "You know what you've done to me, don't you?"

Syd wiggled his backside as he went back through the crawl space. His voice echoed back into the cave. "Something for you to think about while I'm gone."

"Evil fucking goblin," Oberon muttered. "There aren't enough spankings in the world." He settled against the wall and tried not to worry.

He had no idea how much time had passed but the wait seemed interminable. Oberon was on the verge of risking a trip to the surface when rustling and the patter of falling dirt told him someone was coming. Syd appeared through the crawl space, cheeky grin on his face.

"Bored yet?"

Oberon put down the rock he'd been holding. "It felt like you were gone for days."

"Four hours. I had to be sure they were gone. Let's get back to the lodge and I'll tell you what happened."

It was a relief to be above ground even though there was a misty rain falling. The lodge's kitchen was warm and welcoming.

"I've got the fire going in the sitting room," Syd said. "We've got tinned spaghetti and meatballs to eat for a late lunch, followed by shortbread. I'll get the kettle going for tea afterwards."

"Definitely." Oberon rubbed his arms. He'd got colder than he'd thought. He took the dishes of food Syd handed him and went through to the sitting room. The furniture was a mix of mismatched stuff that must have migrated gradually from the castle. There was a thick, tartan rug in front of the fire and Oberon sat on it, leaning against a chair.

Syd arrived with the tin of shortbread. "Found this in a cupboard. Must have been left over from Christmas because it's still in date." They ate in silence. Oberon basked in the warmth of the flames, enjoying the simple meal. When they were finished, Syd cleared the dishes, produced two mugs of hot tea then settled on the rug.

"It was an hour before I saw anything. They came from a mile or so away, several men in a line advancing like beaters on a shoot." Syd gazed into the flames. "I spotted two more coming from the other direction."

"So they were trying to prevent anyone walking out."

"Seems so."

"Did the helicopter come back?"

"Not that I saw. I hope they got really wet feet in the bog."

"They weren't wearing yellow wellies then?"

"They were not." Syd swallowed the last of his tea. "I dressed for hard labour, put the white hat on and went back outside to do some landscaping. We need to add gravel to the front every year because it gets washed away in the winter storms and there had already been a delivery. It seemed best to do something that wasn't a lie, so I walked backwards and forwards with the wheelbarrow, getting more and more dusty. They didn't appear for a while and I was getting tired. I might have a blister!" He examined his palm in disgust.

"I appreciate your sacrifice. I'll kiss it better later."

"Yes, you will." Syd leered. "Just about midday a car came along the track. Three guys got out, acting like they were stopping to stretch their legs or admire the view. Idiots." He picked a piece of shortbread from the tin. "One guy was lean and dark, the other smiled too much. The third was dressed like he was on a grouse shoot. Tweeds and boots—what a prat. He had very bright eyes, like a bird, and seemed annoyed. One of them said good morning. I hadn't looked up when they came over so straightened up like my back hurt then asked if they were lost."

"What did they say?"

"Distraction technique. The older guy said they'd taken a wrong turn then asked if he could use the bathroom. I shrugged and told him to go ahead. He took long enough to have a soak in the bath let alone take a pee. The other two were wandering around having a good look."

"And when he came out?"

"Asked if I'd seen anyone come by this way. I said nobody but them and that the family would be up the next day."

"Clever. Covers any movement for the next twenty-four hours."

"Fran might get curious. Anyway, they all got back in the car then drove off. I kept working and ten minutes later they came back for another look, turned around and sped off. I shovelled gravel for a while longer, came in here to start lunch then walked over to fetch you."

"So we're in the clear?"

"For now, at least. Coming back a third time would be ridiculous."

"I'm not sure I would have been so calm."

"I was paddling like a duck beneath the surface, believe me. They all gave off evil vibes. I don't think having them catch up to you would be fun."

"No." Oberon massaged his temples. "I don't think it would. You did great, so how about I give you a reward?"

"Such as?" Syd batted his lashes.

"I believe you were going to demonstrate how soft this rug is. Get naked while I find supplies."

"In the bedroom. I haven't unpacked my overnight bag yet."

By the time Oberon returned with lube and condoms, Syd was naked and spread on the rug in open invitation. The firelight cast a warm glow on his skin and flames danced in his eyes. Oberon stripped then settled beside him. Their bodies melded together, skin on skin, and they kissed with an intensity that left Oberon fired up for more. He traced Syd's lips with his tongue, delving deeper, tasting him. Syd groaned and Oberon explored his body with gentle caresses. Syd arched and his nipples hardened into peaks.

Oberon broke the kiss, his eyes locked onto Syd's. "Fuck, I want you." He sketched a finger along the curve of Syd's hip then across his belly, teasing. Syd reached for Oberon's erection.

"Why isn't this inside me then? Get with the programme!"

With a growl, Oberon pushed Syd's legs wider apart before positioning himself between them. He struggled with the condom then got lube all over both of them, but finally hoisted Syd's legs onto his shoulders before thrusting into him.

"Gonna get rug burns on my butt," Syd said, grinning.

"Let's hope no sparks spit out of that fire."

"That would bring new meaning to fanning the flames of desire."

"If you've got the head space to crack jokes, I'm not doing this right." Oberon drove into Syd again and again, their bodies slamming together. Syd met each thrust with a moan and demands for more. Oberon didn't hold back. Syd seemed to need it rough and Oberon didn't have the control to go any slower. He drove deep and Syd cried out in ecstasy, his body shaking. The clench of Syd's muscles sent Oberon over the edge, muscles tensing as his orgasm rolled through him and his vision blurred.

"Fuck."

Syd chuckled. "Yep, I think that was what we just did."

Oberon traced a finger along Syd's jawline. "That was...incredible."

"It was."

Oberon was glad Syd didn't reduce the emotion of what had happened with another joke. The moment

was perfect and he wanted the afterglow to last a bit
longer.

Chapter Eight

The next two days at the lodge would have been idyllic if not for the nagging worry at the back of Oberon's mind. He expected men from Black Stone to appear at any moment, or to see the helicopter circling overhead again. Every black speck of a distant bird became a drone in his head. He distracted himself by fucking Syd on every available flat surface and some that weren't so flat. Syd proved to be both flexible and insatiable. He seemed to be enjoying himself just as much as Oberon.

As evening approached, it was getting close to the time they'd have to head south to Syd's godfather. Oberon was glad that they could finally get moving. He wanted to hand responsibility for what he knew over to someone more fit to deal with the information. He was stuffing his pack when Syd stomped in from outside. He didn't look happy.

"What's up?" Oberon asked.

Syd scowled. "We have a problem. I was checking the Mini over and it has two flat tyres. I guess the journey up here did the damage. They must have been slow punctures because I would have noticed otherwise. I only have one spare here."

"Bugger. What are we going to do?"

"I've got a mountain bike in the lean-to. I'll have to cycle back to the castle then get Fran to bring me back in the Land Rover with extra tyres."

"How far is it?"

"Twenty-five miles roughly. It'll take three times as long as it did in the car—you know the state of the roads. We'll have to delay our departure by another day."

"Okay, but I should go. If those men come back again, you'll need to be here, not me."

"You could be right. Can you find your way, though? It was pitch black when we drove up here."

"It's not that complicated," Oberon said. "I think I'll be okay. I've got a decent sense of direction and there's a compass in my pocket I haven't had a chance to use yet."

"Aren't you the Boy Scout?"

"One joke about woggles and I will end you."

"Spoilsport."

"Can we get back to fixing the car situation?"

"Okay, I don't think we have much choice when we both left our phones at the castle. There's very limited signal here anyway. I'll show you a back way into the castle. It cuts about five miles off the journey. It's a bit rough going but the bike can handle it."

"I'll leave straight away. There's an hour or so of light left. I need to make use of it."

Syd rubbed the back of his neck. "I had another thought. What if we didn't get the punctures on the way up here?"

"You mean it could have been our uninvited visitors?"

"Two of them had a good look around while one kept me talking. It wouldn't have been difficult for them to sabotage the Mini. You could be riding into a trap."

Oberon didn't have to think about that for long. "It's a chance we'll have to take. Luck has been on our side so far and we can't cycle all the way to Cumbria. We need the car and we have to get to your godfather."

Syd ran a hand through his hair. "I don't like this. Just be careful, okay?"

"Hey, come here." Oberon pulled Syd into a hug. "I'll be fine. I can look after myself and I have you to get back to, don't I?"

"You do. And I...I like you in one piece."

"You like me, do you?" Oberon teased.

"Don't get full of yourself. I like lots of people. I mean, not in the same way because I'm not a slut, last night's performance notwithstanding, but...oh, you know what I mean!"

"Yes, I think I do."

Half an hour later Oberon was on his way, pedalling as fast as the rough terrain would allow. Syd's mountain bike wasn't designed for distance cycling but it was robust enough to deal with a gravel track full of potholes the size of the Grand Canyon. Oberon wasn't quite as well equipped as the bike. As the light faded, he hit more and more bumps.

The next thing he knew he was coming round, cold and stiff, in pitch blackness. It took him a little while to remember where he was and what he'd been doing. He could see a clear, starry sky through a net of heather, then the dark slope of a hill, and his own boots tangled in a blackberry bush. "What the actual fuck?"

There was liquid dripping into his eye and when he touched his forehead, his fingers came away sticky. The bike was nowhere to be seen. *Must have hit something and got thrown off. Damn.* The darkness meant he had to have been out cold for at least half an hour. A ginger testing of his limbs revealed no significant damage other than a few more cuts and bruises to add to his collection. His head was pounding though, and his neck was stiff. He needed to recover the bike but when he got to his knees to look around, there was no sign of it. Worse, he could see down the valley and there were men below, no more than a quarter of a mile away, spaced out on the hillside like a fan, and beating the heather by torchlight. He didn't have time to search for the bike in the darkness and the small pack he'd brought, containing his waterproof, was strapped to the saddle.

So much for being lucky. Oberon crawled behind a boulder, and from there rolled into a shallow trench which slanted up the mountain face. Following it took him to a narrow gully that allowed him to stay hidden to the top of the next ridge. From there he looked back and the hunters were still patiently quartering the hillside and moving upwards. There was no change of pace to indicate that he'd been spotted.

When he reached the other side of the ridge, he felt safe enough to get to his feet and run. It was hard going and Oberon was sore from his fall. Running wasn't going to get him clear and he was now in sight of the end of the search line. He took a calculated risk and showed himself. Cries drifted on the air and the line of torches changed direction. Keeping low, Oberon doubled back and in twenty minutes made it to the ridge behind his pursuers. There was some satisfaction in seeing them head uphill in the wrong direction but he couldn't rely on them being fooled for long.

He set off in what he thought was the way to the castle with the vague hope of making it there, even though he still had to be ten miles away. He had maybe twenty minutes' start but little knowledge of the area. His compass, which had been in his pocket, had gone. Presumably lost when he came off the bike. In the dark, even by starlight, the going was treacherous and he couldn't help but feel he was being herded. He ran as fast as he dared and got off the ridge onto moorland before any figures appeared on the skyline. He jumped across a brook and came out on a narrow road passing between two glens. It was far too exposed to stay on but after jogging a hundred meters or so a gate appeared and beyond it a gravelled track that had to run to a farm or house. *Somewhere this remote might provide a place to hide. Think I'm out of other options.*

Decision made, he ran, lungs burning, and he didn't look back. He came to an abandoned cottage but with barely three walls remaining, he dismissed it as a possible hiding place and carried on. Panting, he reached the top of a shallow incline and spotted the chimneys of a house in the distance. Leaving the road, he took the most direct route and after stumbling across a stream found himself on a lawn. It was roughly cut and planted with beds of scrubby rhododendrons but definitely marked the edge of the property. The house that appeared out of the darkness might once have been a farm but had been extended. There were several lights on and through the glass windows of a large conservatory, Oberon saw someone standing there, watching him. Someone who beckoned him inside.

Not like I have much choice. Oberon limped to the conservatory door. When he peered inside, he saw the scariest collection of plants he'd ever come across. He spotted several carnivorous varieties he'd seen in jungles around the world. The air was heavy with the scent of exotic blooms and their vibrant colours were brought to life by the starlight filtering through the glass ceiling. Oberon hesitated as he tried to make sense of his surroundings and take stock of the level of danger. The person who had beckoned him inside was nowhere to be seen. A shiver ran down his spine but there was no going back. He could hear the shouts of his hunters getting closer all the time. Steeling himself, he took a cautious step forward, pushing aside a curtain of greenery. Beyond it was a door into the house. The room Oberon stepped into was filled with display cases containing various artifacts that he might have expected to see in a museum. The walls were lined with bookcases. In the middle of it all was a huge desk and seated behind it was the man who had invited Oberon in. An invitation he was already regretting accepting.

It was the middle of the night and the elderly man didn't seem at all bothered by the scruffy stranger who had invaded his home. He was bald and had a round, shiny face. He wore dark-framed glasses, which were perched on the end of his nose and he seemed to be waiting for Oberon to speak.

Lost for words and with a growing feeling of unease, Oberon just stared at him.

"Are you in need of assistance?" the man asked. "My name is Frobisher."

Oberon's guts lurched. He recognized the name from Art's notes. He hoped the semi-darkness concealed his reaction and nodded towards the window. It had a view across the moor and the bobbing lights of torches were clearly visible.

"Ah, I see," Frobisher said. "A fugitive from justice, eh? We can discuss your situation shortly but for now, go through the door on the left over there and close it behind you. You'll be perfectly safe. I object to the police stomping over my property for no good reason."

Oberon did as the man directed, and found himself in a dark store cupboard, which smelt of cleaning supplies, and was lit only by a tiny window high up in the wall. The door swung closed behind him with a click. He wasn't happy. The name could be a coincidence — it wasn't that unusual — but Frobisher had been far too relaxed and ready, almost as if he had expected Oberon's arrival and his eyes had been sharply intelligent. No sound filtered into the cupboard and for all Oberon knew, the police might be searching the house. *How did he know they were police when I didn't know myself?*

There was a click and the door opened. Oberon emerged, blinking in the light, to find his host studying him with blatant curiosity.

"Have they gone?" Oberon asked, attempting an air of calm.

"They have. I convinced them that I had scared you off with a shotgun and that you had crossed the hill. Gun ownership is not uncommon around here. Sheep rustling and equipment theft are big problems. Most landowners keep licensed weapons."

"Why did you do that? Not that I want to seem ungrateful, but you could get into a lot of trouble."

"Because I don't want the police to come between us, Mr. Wycherley." As he spoke, his eyelids dropped over his sharp grey eyes. Oberon remembered Art describing the man he feared most. He had said that he "could hood his eyes like a hawk" and Oberon realised that he had run, or been driven, straight into a trap.

Well fuck. This isn't good. His first impulse was to tackle the old man then make a run for it, but Frobisher seemed to anticipate the intention. He smirked then nodded to the door. Oberon turned and saw two of the men Syd had described seeing at the lodge. Both were holding guns. *I thought there were strict fucking gun laws in this country.*

"You're not going anywhere, Mr. Wycherley, so please relax. You've had a rough evening."

"The police manhunt...you arranged that?"

"Why do the grunt work when you can get others to do it for you? It wasn't difficult to plant the suggestion that a wanted fugitive had been spotted hiding on the moors." He took a step closer then reached out to touch Oberon's hair. Oberon flinched away. "A white hat wasn't an adequate imitation for this, I'm afraid. Your young friend did a good job of covering for you. He hid you well."

"You sabotaged the car then?"

"Of course. It was a calculated guess that you'd need to leave your little hidey hole sooner or later and for that you'd need transport. This house belongs to a...sympathizer. It was simply a matter of encouraging you in this direction, but what happened to your head?"

Oberon said nothing.

"No matter. The moors are full of hazards in the dark."

"What do you want with me?"

"A friendly chat, that's all. My friends and I would like to know how much the American told you. He stayed in your London flat long enough for him to tell you some stories. You've taken us on quite the dance since then and I admit, my patience is wearing thin."

"You killed Art and set me up as a murderer. That's why I ran. Art didn't tell me anything. He needed a place to stay and I helped him out." Plausible deniability felt desperate, but Oberon was all out of ideas.

"Unlikely. I'll enjoy getting the truth out of you, but that pleasure will have to wait a while. I have some less stimulating things to attend to first."

"You can't keep me here."

"Can't I? What exactly are you going to do about it? I think I have the advantage, don't you?"

Oberon took a step towards the door and immediately one of the gunmen grabbed his arm, twisting it behind his back. When he struggled, the other man hit him across the face.

"Who *are* you?" Oberon asked, spitting blood onto the pristine carpet. Frobisher's eyes were cold and malignant. It was hard to look away.

"Put Mr. Wycherley in the guest room until I return, Rownham. Make sure he's on a short leash. I don't want him straying. His comfort is not a priority."

Oberon was marched outside and around the house to an outbuilding. One of his captors, the one Frobisher had called Rownham, heaved open the heavy door then shoved him inside. He was pushed to the floor then handcuffed by one wrist to some metal racking.

Without saying a word, both men left and having locked him in, Oberon could hear them shifting around outside the door. They were talking but in voices too low to hear.

The atmosphere in the storeroom was palpably damp. It was pitch black and the concrete floor was cold. By groping as far as he could reach, Oberon found that the racking was stacked with boxes and barrels. Sacks of something heavy were propped at their base and the whole place smelt of mould and disuse.

Miserable and in pain, he sat in the cold and dark. *I should have taken my chances with the police, though old weird-eyes didn't take long to get rid of them. Probably has some influence. I wonder how long it will be before Syd realises something's wrong.* Oberon didn't know how much time he had before Frobisher began his interrogation but the more he thought about his situation, the angrier he got. *I can't just sit here and do nothing. I can't let them win.* He yanked on the handcuff and to his amazement, the edge of the shelving made an unpleasant grinding noise and shifted slightly. The rusted metal was held together by decaying bolts, many of which were loose. He grabbed the cuffs' short chain with his free hand and pulled as hard as he could. A bolt shot free and bounced across the floor. There was no sign the men outside had heard anything, so Oberon kept tugging. He was rewarded when the entire shelf dropped at one end, launching its contents onto the floor, and he could slide the handcuff free. He froze, expecting his guards to burst through the door at all the racket he was making but nothing happened. *Door must be really thick or they've stepped away a bit.*

He moved around the room, feeling his way in the darkness. He found a window, but it was covered by heavy shutters that were padlocked shut, and there was only the one door. When he investigated the sacks, they seemed to be full of animal feed of some kind. To one side of the room he found, by walking into a sharp corner, a metal cupboard. It was locked but when Oberon pulled at the door handle it seemed flimsy. He got some purchase on the handle by looping the loose end of the handcuffs through it then pulling as hard as he could. The door gave way and Oberon fell backwards. *Just what I need, more fucking cuts and bruises. Hopefully Syd will be willing to kiss them better.* All the yanking on the cuffs wasn't doing his wrist much good either.

After brushing some of the dirt off his trousers, he explored the shelves as best he could. His first find was a box of long matches and by some miracle they were bone dry. He struck a match and in the brief moment of light it showed him a stock of electric torches on one shelf. With a torch to help, he investigated further. He found bottles of chemicals, pesticides and turpentine. Coils of fine copper wire sat next to a box of detonators, and cord for fuses. At the back of a shelf, he found a wooden case. When he wrenched it open, he found half a dozen grey bricks, each a couple of inches square. When he picked one up, it crumbled easily in his hand. *Explosives. With one of these bricks, I could blow this whole place into the atmosphere and probably myself with it.*

Oberon had been trained in the use of explosives, but he was mainly familiar with automation and remote blasting technologies, advanced initiation systems and precision techniques using blast design software. The mining industry had come a long way from dynamite's high energy output and sensitivity. *The storage of this stuff is almost certainly illegal and it could be ancient.* Oberon was between a rock and a hard place. *If I attempt to use this stuff I could blow myself up but if I don't, I'll probably be tortured and killed anyway.* He didn't have to think about it for long. *Fuck it.* He got a detonator and fixed it to a few feet of fuse. Then he took a quarter of a grey brick and put it at the foot of the door, fixing the detonator in it. He would have preferred to bury it but the concrete was solid. He dragged a feed sack on top of it all then moved the box of explosives as far away as possible, burying it under more heavy sacks. He built a low wall with the rest of the feed then got down behind it, took a deep breath and lit the fuse.

There was a surge of pressure, heat, and a blinding flash of light. The wall opposite him exploded outwards and Oberon felt as though he'd been thumped hard in the chest. Something dropped on him, catching his left shoulder, then everything went black.

He wasn't unconscious long because he came round to choking fumes and clouds of dust. Coughing hard, he crawled through scattered debris towards fresh air. A huge rent had been torn in the wall and the door had been ripped apart. Two bodies lay sprawled on the ground, partly covered by debris. Oberon staggered to his feet, stepped outside, bent double then threw up.

"Gross." He spat a few times to clear his mouth then staggered farther away from the house, making his way to the rear of the property. He didn't care if Frobisher's men were dead or alive, just that they wouldn't be coming after him anytime soon.

The outlines of more outbuildings loomed through the smoke. A stream ran through a deep cutting between them. Oberon slid down the bank into the water, rinsed his mouth and washed the grit from his eyes. He squirmed up the other side and made his way to the first structure, coming across a trap door that must once have granted access to a beer or grain cellar. He heaved it up and slid inside.

The building had obviously been out of use for a long time. The wooden floor was rotten and half the roof was missing. Oberon lay on his back and gazed at the stars through the jagged teeth of splintered beams. A plume of smoke drifted across his view, bringing him back to reality. Nausea churned his guts and his left shoulder and arm throbbed.

I can't stay here. They'll find me in no time once they realise I didn't blow myself up. I need somewhere to hide where I can rest and recover a while. He was in no condition to run but guessed his enemies would assume that he would make for open country. The darkness was his friend as he clambered out of the cellar then made his way across a cobbled yard. He heard cries from the direction of the house and there was smoke issuing from an upstairs window, backlit by an orange glow. He allowed himself a brief smile. *Something from the explosion must have hit the house. All those chemicals. That'll keep them busy for a while.*

In the field closest to the back of the house, he spotted a dovecot. It seemed like the perfect hiding spot. Its weathered wood and overgrown ivy offered refuge as he slipped inside. The cooing of the doves masked his laboured breathing as he settled in the corner, his heart still racing from his self-inflicted brush with death. From his vantage point, he could see shadows moving frantically around the burning house, their shouts carried by the wind. As he listened intently, a faint sound caught his attention—the fluttering of wings above him. Looking up, he saw a lone dove perched on a beam, its eyes fixed on him as if assessing his presence. Beyond the dove, Oberon spotted a stone parapet that supported the network of beams. *If I can get up there I'd be well hidden. Has to be worth a try.*

With his injured arm it wasn't easy, but Oberon managed the climb somehow by using jutting stones, gaps in the masonry and some tough ivy roots. There was just enough room for him to lie out beyond the parapet, completely hidden from anyone below. Relief that he hadn't fallen didn't last long. Feeling sick, his head pounding, Oberon drifted into unconsciousness once more.

He awoke with the worst headache he could ever remember having. His shoulder was immoveable, his arm hanging. Outside it was light but the sun was low enough to tell him that it was still early. Through one of the dove holes, he examined the yard and gardens beneath but there was no sign of movement. *Need to move. If I die up here, I'll be mummified before anyone finds me.*

The descent from his hiding place proved to be even more challenging than the climb up. He slithered the last few feet and had a rough enough landing to make him bite his tongue to stop from screaming in pain. He sat in the dirt for a while, psyching himself up to move then, without any kind of plan in his aching head, he made his way around the house. He thought he might be able to find a phone or some kind of transport he could steal. The place seemed abandoned and his confidence that he was alone grew. *Where have they all gone? Fuck, I don't care, I just want to get out of here.* He limped to the garage, which was more of a car port, open along the front. It housed a tractor, a sleek BMW and a rusting Volvo. The keys were all hanging on pegs on a side wall.

Oberon went for the Volvo. The tractor might have blended in with the landscape better but would have been too slow and he'd never driven one before. The Volvo was less ostentatious than the BMW. In a car, he could be at Syd's family seat in half an hour. Oberon's relief when the car started first time made him laugh. *Now I just have to hope that there are no more obstacles between me and the castle.*

Chapter Nine

"Oberon, what the hell did you do to yourself? You look like hammered shit."

"Fran?" Oberon was a bit woozy but still had enough mental capacity to wonder why he was staring down the barrel of a shotgun. "Are you going to shoot me, cos I already had a rough night?"

Fran lowered the barrel. "Whose car is this? Where's Syd? Why do you look like you were in an explosion?"

"Because I was. In an explosion, I mean. I stole the car. Syd is still at the lodge. I hope."

"Fuck! Get out of the damned car. How did you drive here in that condition?"

"Not sure to be honest. Don't remember most of it. Might need a hand." Oberon had the impression he was slurring his words, but his head hurt too much to be sure.

"Christ on a stick." Fran put the gun on the ground before helping Oberon out of the car. His knees buckled but she propped him up then steered him into the castle. Somehow, he'd managed to drive all the way to the front door. With not inconsiderable effort and a lot of cursing, she got him into a chair in the kitchen. "Don't keel over in the next five minutes, I need to go retrieve the gun."

Nodding hurt. Oberon slumped over the table, resting his head on the one arm he could move without screaming. Sheer force of will kept him conscious. As soon as Fran came back, he said, "Syd needs tyres for the Mini at the lodge. He'll be worried sick by now. I should have been here late last night but I ran into a few…issues."

Fran stood with her hands on her hips. "You two are all kinds of trouble, aren't you? Right, I won't ask any more. I'll get you to Syd's room so you can lie down then head out to the lodge. Do you need a doctor?"

"That's not a good idea. I'll manage. Just get Syd. Things are heating up and we need to head south as soon as possible."

Swearing under her breath about male incompetence, Fran helped Oberon to Syd's tower room. She left him sitting on the edge of the bed with instructions not to answer a phone, go to the door for any reason, or die. Oberon didn't think he could manage either of the first two but felt it best not to argue. The third was a possibility. His relief at his escape was clouded by pain. He had a crushing headache, and still felt sick. His shoulder was in a bad way.

He struggled out of his clothes, leaving them in a filthy heap on the floor. *They'll have to be incinerated.* The main bathroom was too far away to contemplate the journey so Syd's tiny sink had to do. Oberon filled it with cool water then used a washcloth to get a bit cleaner. He let his head hang and watched blood and dirt stain the water as it circled the drain. Syd's bed was calling so Oberon patted himself dry. Even the soft towel was too painful to rub against his damaged skin. He dragged his feet the short distance to the bed, collapsed onto it and that was all he knew until voices penetrated his consciousness.

"Get out, Fran, he's naked!" Syd's voice was way too loud.

"It's not like I haven't seen a naked man before, Syd. Don't be a spoilsport. Oh, wow! Maybe I haven't seen a naked *man* before. Not bad, little brother."

"Out!" There were sounds of scuffling then the click of the door.

"Woz goin' on?" Oberon's tongue was apparently made of foam rubber and his eyelids were superglued shut.

"Sorry, I didn't mean to wake you but my pain-in-the-rear sister was getting an eyeful of your booty."

"Huh?"

"I guess you were so exhausted you collapsed onto the bed without getting under the covers."

"Yeah..." Oberon had vague memories of washing but nothing after that. "Sorry." Groaning, he wriggled beneath the covers.

"You're pretty banged up for someone that was only supposed to be fetching tyres, mister."

"Didn't quite go to plan." Oberon managed to open his eyes. "What time is it?"

"Three in the afternoon. Fran said you got here early, around seven."

"She pointed a gun at me. A big one."

"She does that."

"So, I've been out for a few hours?"

"It took a while for her to get to me, get the new tyres on the Mini, which she did while I supervised, then drive back here."

"Did you pass anyone?"

"A fire engine heading towards Dougal McLeish's house. He's an asshole, so I hope it burned to the ground."

"Bit late. The fire started in the early hours."

"And you know this because…"

"I may have set off some explosives and I'm guessing that was the place."

Syd stared at him. "No shit? That's so cool!"

"I worry about you."

"How do you think I felt when you didn't come back last night?"

Oberon sat up then wished he hadn't. "Fuck. Got an aspirin?"

"Lie on your front, idiot. I'll fetch the first aid kit."

An hour later, Syd had patched grazes, glued cuts and extracted splinters. Most of Oberon's body had been doused in arnica, antiseptic and burn cream.

"I smell weird."

"Quit whining. You're a mess. What happened to your shoulder?"

"Got hit with something in the explosion. Don't know what, I was busy ducking."

"At least it didn't whack you in the head. You should get seen at a hospital. There's a deep cut and a nasty burn."

"We both know that's not an option."

"Once you're dressed, I'll put your arm in a sling. It'll stop the wound reopening every time you move."

"Okay. You're pretty good at this stuff."

"I was an excellent sea cadet."

"That takes my mind to places it definitely shouldn't go."

"Like a man in uniform, huh? I have a fancy dress fireman's outfit somewhere, in case you're interested."

"Another time, Syd."

"You think you can make it downstairs? Fran was putting a meal together and she'll want to know everything. It'll save you going through your story twice."

Oberon dosed himself with the strongest painkillers Syd could find then dressed. Syd tied a sling and it was a huge relief when it took the weight off Oberon's injured shoulder. Syd still kept an arm around his waist all the way to the kitchen. Oberon was sweating by the time he got into a chair.

"I realise it's late afternoon, but I thought we could all do with a decent meal," Fran said, serving bowls of chicken casserole with herb dumplings and chunks of crusty bread. "Casserole solves most problems, in my opinion."

Oberon worried his nausea might return but his stomach growled in anticipation. His headache was less hammer drill and more dull throb since he'd taken the meds. After the first mouthful of food stayed in his stomach, he set to with relish and was soon scraping the bowl clean. "Thanks, Fran, that was fantastic."

"Yeah, not bad, sis. Is there any left?" Syd looked hopefully at the stove.

"Not for you and definitely not for Obi until I hear all about last night."

"Get talking," Syd ordered. "My stomach is relying on you."

Oberon related the events of the previous night as best he could remember. Fran stared at him wide-eyed while Syd scowled.

"The man you described, with the scary eyes, Frobisher, that's not Dougal McLeish using a different name. Dougal must have lent those people his house. He always was an obnoxious bastard. More right-wing than Mussolini."

"What the hell was he doing with explosives on his premises?" Fran asked.

"There's an old quarry on his land, isn't there?" Syd suggested. "Probably dates back to when that was active. You were lucky the stuff was still there, Obi."

"Not sure about lucky. Desperate, maybe. I didn't want to find out what Frobisher's questioning techniques might involve."

"These are nasty people, that's for sure." Syd tilted his chair back. "We'll have to head south tonight."

Fran slapped Syd around the head. "Obi isn't in a fit condition to travel."

"Even so, we have to go. It's vital we move quickly."

"He's right, Fran," Oberon said. "I don't see how I can get more proof of what's going on than I've already got. Your godfather can believe me, or not. Whatever he decides, I'll be safer than I am now. I can handle a car ride."

Fran glared at him, then at her brother. "I can see I'm not going to change your minds. I'll put some food together, make you a flask of coffee and sort some first aid supplies." Decision made, she got to work.

Syd grabbed his and Oberon's bowls and went over to the stove to get refills.

"How long will it take us to get there?" Oberon asked, tucking in.

"Eight or nine hours," Syd replied. "That's if there are no hold ups. With a stop or two, we should get there by three in the morning."

"Surely your godfather won't appreciate us appearing in the early hours?"

"He's had my letter and I'll call him from a payphone when we stop for a break. He's always been a night owl. Don't worry about it."

Oberon shrugged and immediately regretted it. "On your head be it. Will you be able to drive that far? I'm not going to be much help."

"Appropriate amounts of caffeine and sugar and I could drive to the moon." Syd grinned.

"I'd rather we didn't go *that* far."

"Oh, we can go all the way...whenever you like."

"Stop it you two," Fran exclaimed. "My ears are burning. Syd. Go pack overnight bags for both of you and try to remember toothbrushes as well as condoms and lube."

"You two are gonna make me die from embarrassment, aren't you?" Oberon moaned.

"If you don't kill yourself first," Fran retorted, "because you seem to be trying really hard to do that."

Within the hour, they were on the road. The Mini was equipped with new tyres and a fresh spare. Syd had insisted that Oberon recline his seat to get some more rest and his battered body was cushioned with pillows. He slept hard, waking only when Syd pulled into a garage to get fuel.

"Aren't we on the motorway?" Oberon mumbled, peering out of the window.

"I thought we'd be less likely to be spotted if I avoided big service stations with loads of security cameras. I pulled off at the last junction."

"Good idea. I think you're better at this skullduggery stuff than I am."

"Skullduggery? You sound like a fifteenth century pirate." Syd chuckled. "I could be your captive cabin boy. I can picture you in thigh boots and a frilly shirt."

"What about trousers?"

"Not essential." With that parting shot, Syd got out to refuel then disappeared into the tiny shop. He came back laden with snacks and caffeine-loaded drinks. "Fran packed healthy stuff for us. Yuck. This is much better. It's time you took some more painkillers. How are you doing?"

"Fine. Thinking about pirates thanks to you."

"You want to sleep more, or sit up?"

"Sit. You must be tired and I can help keep you awake."

Syd ran around the car so he could crank Oberon's seat up then returned to the driver's seat. He pulled off the forecourt and drove to the next layby. "I need to eat and drink. Multitasking while driving is not one of my many talents and you've been in enough crashes recently." He opened a bottle of water then handed it over. "I got you the lame stuff. Take your pills."

Oberon looked on while Syd consumed enough sugar to down a diabetic elephant and so much caffeine he'd be climbing the walls for the next three nights at least. When they got back on the road, Syd didn't stop talking. Oberon relaxed into his seat and accepted that he'd be doing the listening for the next few hours.

As it got later, the motorway got emptier. Syd kept strictly to the speed limit in case of lurking unmarked police cars. When he finally took the exit for the Lakes, Oberon was hurting everywhere. The roads were much twistier from then on and the journey got progressively more uncomfortable. He was relieved when they finally reached the village of Hawkshead, where Syd's godfather had his holiday home.

"Mo's place is on the edge of the village," Syd said. "Quite isolated and very private. He likes it that way."

"Should I be worried about meeting him?"

"He can be a bit intimidating, I guess, but I'm his favourite godson, obviously. You'll be fine."

"I'm so reassured."

"Well, we're here so it's a bit late to get squeamish."

Syd drove down a short, narrow lane before pulling up in front of whitewashed cottage. There was a man standing at the door.

Syd got out of the car then went around to help Oberon out. He gritted his teeth at the pain as his shoulder protested but tried not to let it show just how much he was hurting. Syd bounded over to the door.

"Uncle Mo! It's so good to see you." Hugs were exchanged, then Mo turned his attention to Oberon.

"Mr. Wycherley, I understand you've been having quite the adventure. I'm Mo Stanley."

"Yes, sir. We've been busy."

"And you look like you're about to fall over. After Syd called me from the road, I took the opportunity to bring in a doctor friend of mine. He's waiting inside to take a look at you. Don't worry, he's very discreet."

Mo was a striking man with pure white hair and light blue eyes. Not quite as tall as Oberon, he had a solid frame and broad shoulders. "Syd, take your friend to the guest bedroom."

"Aunt Ella…is she around?"

"Staying with a friend in Keswick for a few days. There's no one else in the house, just some security staff in the grounds."

Inside, Syd led the way along a passage and up a staircase to a bedroom with floral wallpaper and thick velvet drapes. There was a man waiting, his shirtsleeves rolled up, doctor's bag on the bed. He took one look at Oberon and frowned.

"I'm Dr. Seymour, you can call me Arthur. Clothes off. On the bed."

"That's my line," Syd muttered.

"Syd, make yourself scarce, or I'll tell your friend about the time you went skinny dipping in the lake and got bitten in a sensitive place by a defensive goose."

"What happened to doctor patient confidentiality, doc?" Syd pouted but backed out of the room.

"Sacrificed when you scrumped my apples, young man." The doctor shut the door on Syd's spluttering response. "That boy is incorrigible."

Oberon thought it best to do as he was ordered. The doctor was gentle but thorough. He muttered at Syd's first aid efforts but eventually told Oberon he could get dressed. "You're young and fit, there's nothing that won't heal. Syd didn't do too bad a job on your shoulder, apart from being a bit generous with the surgical glue. Stitches would have been better. Your burns are no doubt sore, but superficial. I'll give you some prescription painkillers and a better sling, which I think I have in the car. You'll need to keep the arm immobile for a few days, then start gentle exercises."

"Thanks, doctor."

"Arthur. When you're ready, Sir Morris will see you in the lounge." He put a bottle of tablets on the bed then left Oberon alone.

I guess this is it. He'll believe me or not. Oberon winced as he struggled into his clothes. *I'm not running anymore, I'm too fucking tired.*

Before he went downstairs, Oberon found a bathroom. His reflection wasn't easy viewing. *I look like I've gone a few rounds with Mike Tyson. Perhaps I should let a beard grow to cover some of the damage.* He rubbed a finger over his emerging stubble then shook his head. *Better to look battered than thirty years older.* He freshened up a little but didn't want to keep his host waiting too long.

He limped down the stairs and followed the sounds of voices to a cosy sitting room. Syd was lounging on the couch, a tumbler of gold-coloured liquid in his hand. "Hey, Obi, the doc gave you a good report on his way out. He left you a new sling." Syd made to get up but Morris told him to stay put. He put the padded foam sling around Oberon's arm, making sure it was comfortable.

"Take a seat, Mr. Wycherley. I won't offer you a drink on Arthur's orders and I'm not going to keep you up long. You need sleep more than anything and your story can keep until morning."

"It's Oberon, and I appreciate your hospitality, sir, but I can't stay under your roof on false pretences. Has Syd told you that I'm wanted by the police?"

"He hasn't given you away but you don't need to worry, not anymore, and call me Morris, or Mo."

"I don't understand." Oberon wondered if the stronger pain meds were messing with his ability to think straight.

"I'll explain more tomorrow, but suffice to say that you're no longer on the list of suspects for the Portland Place murder."

"I don't know what to say...has the killer been caught?"

"Unfortunately not, but I want the two of you to get some rest for what remains of the night. You're perfectly safe here. My position merits a certain amount of security. I'm afraid there's only the one guest bedroom. Syd can sleep in here on the couch."

"I can't believe you said that with a straight face, Uncle Mo!" Syd swallowed his drink. "You know damn well we're together."

"Did it cross your mind, Syd, that Oberon is injured and might appreciate a bed to himself?"

"He won't...will you?" Syd turned beseeching puppy eyes on Oberon.

"You can sleep in the bed, though with the amount of sugar and caffeine you've consumed I'd be surprised if you can sleep at all."

Syd yawned so wide that his jaw cracked. "I'm frazzled. Put me in a bed and I'll sleep."

"I'll leave you two to sort yourselves out then. It's long past my bedtime and we have a lot to talk about tomorrow." Mo gave Syd's shoulder a squeeze before heading for the stairs.

"He's not fazed by anything, is he?" Oberon said.

Syd grinned. "Are you surprised? You don't get his job by being easily shocked. Are you sure you don't mind sharing? I can manage with the couch if you want the space."

"I want you in my bed, Syd. I'm floating on a very nice narcotic cloud right now. I could sleep with an orangutan and not notice."

"I think I should be offended but I'm too tired to bother about being compared to a big, hairy ape." Syd took Oberon's hand. "Let's go. You can dream about me giving you a good time."

"Now I'm off the Met's most wanted list, I might just do that."

"Isn't that great?"

"It's a massive relief. I want to know how and why."

"Tomorrow. Actually, it's tomorrow already, but any sleep is better than none."

"Don't let me sleep in, okay? We need to tell your godfather everything as soon as possible. I'm surprised he wants to wait."

Syd stripped then scrambled into bed. "Quit worrying. I gave him the basics while you were getting prodded by the doc. If he wanted to talk before the morning, he would have said so."

Oberon undressed then joined Syd in bed. He shifted until he got reasonably comfortable. "Okay. Not sure my brain's working properly anyway." He yawned.

"You hooked up with me. I think it's working fine." Syd's words tailed off and seconds later he was snoring. Oberon lay there a while longer, trying not to think at all.

* * * *

The following morning, after a huge breakfast produced by Mo's housekeeper who'd walked over from the village, they all convened in Mo's study.

"I have man cave envy," Syd muttered.

"Me too," Oberon agreed. The room was untidy but comfortable. There were books everywhere, watercolour paintings of Lakeland scenes covered the walls and there was a well-stocked drinks cabinet in a corner. Mo settled behind his sizeable desk, which was cluttered with knick-knacks, while Syd and Oberon occupied the two armchairs in front of it.

"How about we begin with you telling me your story, Oberon. From the beginning," Mo suggested.

Oberon was a little nervous beneath Mo's shrewd gaze but recounted his version of events. He told him about London, about Art Carew and his notebook. He described Art's prediction about the planned murder of Kairos Doukas. Then he got to finding Art's body and the escape from London. He skipped over what he and Syd had gotten up to on the Caledonian sleeper train, saying only that they met on the journey. Being hunted around Scotland by mysterious enemies sounded ridiculous even as he told the story, but Mo didn't laugh or question his account. In fact, he grew steadily more serious. Oberon was a bit reticent about admitting to blowing up a house, but it had been necessary.

"And then Syd drove us here. That's everything." Oberon stilled, worried about how Mo might react.

"That's quite a story," Mo said.

"Not a story, it's the truth," Oberon said. "I wish it weren't."

"I apologise. I didn't mean to imply that I didn't believe you. Do you still have the notebook?"

Oberon laid the book on the desk. "I think I deciphered the code it's written in."

"Excellent. That'll save some time. You should know that I received a letter from Art Carew on the thirty-first of May. Your story confirms much of what he said."

"But he'd been dead a week by then," Oberon said.

"The letter was written and posted on the twenty-third. The opening line was that he was probably dead."

"He did tell me he'd sent a letter to MI5, come to think of it. At the time I wasn't sure he was telling the truth. What else did he say?"

"The same story he gave you. It wouldn't usually have reached my desk but the name Frobisher alerted the agent who opened it. That name had been flagged for my attention. We've had other intelligence about Mr. Selwyn Frobisher and his colleagues."

"Art knew they were after him. He was scared."

"Well he said he'd found shelter with a good friend. When his body was found, we joined the dots and assumed you were that friend. Inquiries suggested it was highly unlikely that you were his killer. The police were trying to find you, Oberon, but to bring you to me, not to arrest you. When I got Syd's letter I felt it best to let things run their course."

"So you knew about me before I escaped from London?"

Mo nodded. "We did."

Oberon stared at Syd. "I'm beginning to think that meeting you on that train wasn't so much of a coincidence. Is Syd even your godson?"

"Oh yes, but he's also my employee."

Oberon went cold. He directed his gaze to Syd. "You're a fucking MI5 agent?"

"Yeah, sorry about that." Syd had the grace to blush.

Clenching the fist that wasn't in a sling, Oberon got to his feet. "I need some air." He went to the door. "I can't believe I was so stupid."

"Obi, wait!" Syd called out but Oberon needed some alone time. He'd been used and it wasn't a nice feeling. He'd not been so close to crying since he was a kid.

He stepped outside into another world. Mo's cottage garden was chocolate-box pretty, stuffed with flowers that attracted swarms of bees and butterflies. There was a heady perfume in the air. Oberon leaned against the stone wall of the building, trying to process what he'd been told. *I can't believe I was so easily manipulated. I thought Syd liked me as much as I like him. I trusted him with my life.*

As he stood there, lost in thought, Mo emerged from the cottage, his expression unreadable. He walked over to Oberon and stood beside him, gazing out at the view of distant fells. After a few moments of silence, Mo spoke. "I know this is a lot to take in, Oberon. But you have to understand, we didn't have a choice. The situation is more complicated than you realize."

Oberon turned to look at him. "Complicated how?"

"There are powerful forces at play here. Very dangerous, powerful people with an agenda that they'll stop at nothing to achieve. Syd was placed in your path for a reason. He was there to keep you alive."

He could have done that without letting me fuck him. "I don't like being kept in the dark, Mo. If I'm going to carry on being involved in whatever this is, I need to know the truth."

"I wish I could tell you everything, Oberon. But there are dangers lurking that you can't even begin to imagine. Your safety, and the safety of those around you, depends on your willingness to trust us."

His words sent a chill down Oberon's spine, but he had little choice. Reluctantly, he nodded. "Fine. I'll trust you…for now. Because I don't have any other options, do I?"

Mo's expression softened and a flicker of relief passed over his features. "You could also consider cutting Syd some slack. He was following orders, but even an old man like me can see he's fallen for you. It's written all over him. You and he can talk later but now, I'd like to take a look at Art's notebook."

Oberon straightened. *There are more important things going on than my bruised ego. Sulking isn't going to help.* Art's notebook was still a welcome distraction because Oberon didn't think he could look Syd in the eye just yet. He followed Mo inside and to his relief, Syd had made himself scarce.

It took a while to work through Art's notes. Oberon explained how he'd worked out the code. Mo grasped it quickly and sat reading and jotting notes. When he was done, his expression was grave.

"I agree with your translation on the whole, Oberon. You did an excellent job." He shook his head. "Mr. Carew got tangled up in a situation he had no business being anywhere near."

"And he paid the ultimate price," Oberon said.

"Indeed. Unfortunately, I think it was inevitable. He was playing a dangerous game and these people are ruthless. Art got the basics right, but the timeline has escalated. Probably thanks to you, Oberon. This group, for whatever reason, has brought their plans forward."

"Is that a good or bad thing?"

"Good for us. Something that's been years in the making doesn't adjust well in the final stages. They will be prone to mistakes."

"I think they have powerful friends. You saw the names. Are they who I think they are?"

"It's likely. They certainly have influence because the business meeting that Mr. Doukas is attending is now the day after tomorrow."

"Can't you stop him coming?" Oberon suspected he knew the answer.

"That wouldn't be a good idea. As far as we know, the individuals after you are unaware you've reached me. They probably think you're still evading them in the wilds of Scotland. That gives us an advantage."

"Are these Black Stone people on your radar?" Oberon asked. "Because it all seems a bit melodramatic."

"It's not a known group, though some of the individuals involved in it are on our radar." Mo said. "Could be a name that Art made up."

"I don't think so." Oberon explained the link he'd found to Islam.

"Hmm. Interesting." Mo paced his study.

"So, what happens next?"

"I go to London to make some arrangements," Mo said. "You need to take some time to recover. I've taken the liberty of arranging for you and a bodyguard to be booked into a secluded hotel. All expenses paid."

"I don't need a bodyguard."

"I'm afraid you do. You've caused these Black Stone people, whoever they are, significant trouble. You really think they'll stop coming after you? You, Mr. Wycherley, are a very annoying loose end for them. You've seen faces, heard names. They'll definitely want to get their hands on you and finish what they started in Scotland. The bodyguard is not negotiable."

Oberon flinched. Mo spoke an unpleasant truth. "No, I guess not." He sighed. "So where am I going?" He shifted his arm in its sling, the pain reminding him of how narrow his escape had been.

"I left it to your bodyguard to sort a place. The fewer people know where you are the better. He'll be here with a car this afternoon."

"Okay." It was a bit deflating to be taken out of the equation.

"I'm ordering you to rest, Oberon." Mo patted his good shoulder. "You've been through a lot. His Majesty's government will no doubt express appreciation at some point but for now, run up an enormous room service bill, sleep, watch bad TV."

It didn't sound too bad. "I'll do my best. I appreciate you looking after me. I don't mean to sound ungrateful. I guess the adrenaline hasn't gone away yet."

"You're exceptionally calm considering what you've been through. I need to get a move on. I'm going to take the notebook with me so our experts can take a look."

Oberon nodded. "Sure. Take care of Mr. Doukas, won't you? From what Art said he seems like one of the good guys."

"I'll do my best to. Try not to worry."

And with that he was gone. Oberon went to find the kitchen to see if he could scrounge a mug of tea or make one himself. *From now on it's a waiting game. Not great at that, but the headspace will be welcome. And some physical distance from Syd, I suppose. I should never have let him get so close.*

Chapter Ten

When Oberon went to the guest bedroom to pack his few things ready to leave, Syd's belongings were already gone. It hurt that he hadn't said goodbye, even if Oberon had no idea what he would have said to him.

How could he? "You're an idiot. He was just doing his job." *And if you hadn't been influenced by your dick, you might have worked it out.* Now he knew the truth, there had been so many signs that Syd was more than he appeared. He'd shared very little about himself on the train journey but asked a lot of questions; he'd tracked Oberon down to Ed's cottage; he handled the visitors at the lodge without any sign of concern…it all added up to someone with an interesting set of skills. "And if you hadn't been so concerned with saving your own skin, you would have asked more questions. Civil servant, my ass. I wonder if Fran knows what he does for a living." Oberon continued muttering to himself as he packed. Being one-handed was frustrating but he recognised that his bad temper had more to do with

Syd than the occasional dropped sock. *He can't have been acting the whole time…I spanked him, for fuck's sake, and he definitely enjoyed it. There's no faking that. Pretty sure that wasn't part of his job description, either.*

Packing done, he stretched out on the bed for a nap. He needed a lot more sleep but his busy mind didn't allow more than a doze. He kept thinking over everything he knew from Art's notebook and wondered how Mo would go about protecting Kairos Doukas. *Art thought nothing could be done to save him but surely there's a way.*

At midday he gave up and ventured downstairs. In the kitchen, Mo's housekeeper gave him a bowl of soup and some crusty bread followed by homemade Victoria sponge. Oberon made polite small talk with her while he ate at the kitchen table. He was about done when the housekeeper, peering out of the window, let him know that his car had arrived.

"Thank you. And for the lunch. That cake was the best I've ever had."

The housekeeper beamed and put another slice in a paper bag for him. "To keep you going. You need feeding up."

"That's amazing." Oberon gave her a hug. He'd left his overnight bag in the hall so grabbed it then walked out to where the vehicle had pulled up. It was a four-wheel drive with mud spattered sides, something that would fit right in to the scenery in the area. The windows were heavily tinted but Oberon could make out the shape of the driver. He put his bag onto the back seat, then open the front passenger door.

"Syd?" Oberon stared at his 'bodyguard'.

"Hey, Obi." Syd gave him a tentative smile. "Get in."

Oberon hesitated then sighed. "Fine." He clambered into the vehicle but struggled with his seatbelt. Syd leaned across to click it into place. He smelled of something fresh and herbal. Oberon kept his sight line directed forwards.

Syd drove down the lane away from the cottage then through the village. He muttered, "Package collected," and Oberon realized he was wearing an earpiece.

"So I'm a package, am I?" Oberon asked, mildly offended.

"That is so open to an inappropriate response," Syd said, straight faced.

"Is someone listening to you?"

"Not anymore." Syd pulled out his earpiece then dropped it into the door pocket. "That message will be passed along to Uncle Mo. He wanted to be sure you'd go with me."

"So this was his idea?"

"Make up with the boy, Sydenham. He'll be good for you. His words, not mine. He seems to think I need to be taken in hand and that you're the man to do it. He likes you, therefore I am well and truly fucked."

Oberon chuckled at Syd's blunt honesty. Uncle Mo orchestrating a reconciliation between him and Syd was beyond unexpected.

"Did he have a back-up plan if I refused?"

"No. He's a good judge of character. I'd have had to kidnap you."

"He did tell me to cut you some slack."

"Listen, Obi," Syd began, "I know you must hate me, and I'm probably the last person you want to spend time with, but I want to make things right between us."

"I don't hate you. I'm not a three year old having a temper tantrum."

"I wouldn't have slept with you on that train if I hadn't genuinely liked you. Promise."

"It wasn't part of your brief to get close to me?"

"Nope. Just to find out where you were going and keep tabs on you. Then later on, to keep you out of your enemies' hands. Didn't make a very good job of that, did I?"

"I don't think you can blame yourself for that."

"Maybe not, but I still feel responsible. I should've seen it coming, should've been there to protect you." Syd's grip on the steering wheel tightened as he navigated the winding road up into the hills.

Oberon studied Syd's profile, the strong line of his jaw set in determination. Despite everything that had happened, he couldn't deny the powerful connection tugging at his heart. "We all make mistakes, Syd. What matters now is what we do next."

They lapsed into silence, unspoken words hanging in the air. As they reached the crest of a hill, a breath-taking view unfolded in front of them — a vast expanse of grey-green fells tipped with gold. A ribbon of lake glinted silver in the far distance. Syd pulled into a view point and turned off the engine. He shifted to face Oberon, his expression earnest. "I want to make amends, Obi. I want to earn your trust back, if you'll let me. I know it won't be easy, but I'm willing to try. I care about you more than I thought possible. I hate that my stupid job might have ruined something brilliant."

Oberon met Syd's gaze, seeing sincerity and vulnerability swirling in those deep blue eyes. Despite the feelings of hurt and betrayal that lingered, a flicker of hope sparked. Maybe, just maybe, they *could* find a way back to each other if they both wanted it enough. *I do want it.*

Oberon reached out and placed a hand on Syd's. The warmth of the connection was a wake-up call. "I don't know that there's anything to forgive. I'm willing to give us a chance. What we have is worth a lot more than bearing a stupid grudge. If I'm honest with myself, I used *you* on that train. I booked a double cabin deliberately to deceive the police and you helped with the charade."

A tentative smile quirked at the corners of Syd's lips as he squeezed Oberon's hand gently. "We're both as bad as each other then. You know, when I first met you on that train, I never expected things to turn out like this."

"Life has a way of surprising us, doesn't it?"

"It certainly does," Syd agreed, his gaze lingering on Oberon. "I never thought I'd find myself caring so deeply for someone...especially someone as bossy as you."

"You know, before all this started, a good friend of mine told me to find myself a cute twink who likes getting his ass spanked."

"Not sure I qualify as a twink," Syd said, "but the spanking bit is right. You have wise friends."

"I never did like that label. I'll take you to meet Marley one day, he's very philosophical about most things. You'll like him."

Syd lowered his window. The air that flooded the car was cool and crisp, carrying with it the earthy scent of the fells. "I love the smell out here. It always seems clean...not surprising, considering the amount of rain this area gets."

"So, where are we headed?" Oberon finally asked. "Mo said he left it to you to pick the hotel."

Syd's eyes sparkled with mischief as he glanced at Oberon. "I thought we could use a change of scenery. I've booked us a room at a quaint old place on a hill above the lake shore. It's quiet, secluded, and far away from prying eyes." He grinned. "It's also really expensive."

Oberon felt a flutter of anticipation at the thought of spending time alone with Syd. "Your godfather is going to rip you a new one."

"Worth it. He said to take good care of you so that's what I'm doing. Obeying orders like a good little spy."

"I should have asked you what kind of civil servant you were, shouldn't I?"

"I wouldn't have been able to tell you. Not then."

"No, I guess not. Does Fran know what you do?"

"No. Nor do my parents. Uncle Mo is Dad's best friend from university. If he found out what kind of career Mo dragged me into, he'd kill him and feed his body to the wolves."

"There are wolves on your estate?"

"Yeah, we're part of a reintroduction programme. They're very cool."

"You didn't mention that when I was cycling back there."

"They wouldn't have eaten you. Maybe taken a little nibble…"

"What about Fran's chickens?"

Syd chuckled. "The wolves have a fenced enclosure. It's massive, but the chickens are safe."

The drive took a while and when they arrived, the hotel proved to be as charming as Syd had described. The old building had ivy crawling up its stone walls and window boxes overflowing with blooms. Syd parked in a space near the door. "We're to stay here until I get word from Uncle Mo that the business with Doukas is over. It'll probably be a couple of days."

"Did you book two rooms?" Oberon asked.

Syd bit his lip. "Uh, no."

"That was presumptuous."

"I'm sure they'll have another. If you want, I can…"

"No."

"No?"

"Can't really spank your misbehaving backside if it's in another room, can I?"

"Uh no." Syd gulped. "We should go check in."

"Yes, we should." Oberon got out of the car. "Suddenly I'm looking forward to the evening."

Syd grabbed their bags then they went inside. As they approached the check-in desk, Oberon brushed Syd's lower back with his hand, continuing over the swell of his backside. Syd froze momentarily until Oberon nudged him.

"Stop that," Syd muttered.

"I don't think so," Oberon replied, enjoying himself.

The receptionist smiled at them as they reached the counter. Her name badge told them she was called Moira. "Welcome to the Silver Moon Hotel. How can I assist you today?"

"We have a reservation under the name Harry Palmer," Syd announced.

"Ah, yes, Mr. Palmer. We have a deluxe suite reserved for you." Moira handed over the key card. "I hope you enjoy your stay with us, gentlemen. Do let me know if there's anything I can help you with."

Oberon took the key card then tucked it into his pocket so he could intertwine his fingers with Syd's as they made their way to the elevator. Once inside, with the door closed, he pressed Syd against the wall. Syd dropped their bags, which landed with a thud.

"I hope you're ready for a night you won't forget," Oberon whispered in Syd's ear. "Or should I call you Harry now?"

"*The Ipcress File* is one of my favourite films, okay?" Syd's voice was shaky. He didn't try to escape.

"Michael Caine is great in it, but I don't want to talk about your film viewing preferences right now." As the elevator door dinged open to their floor, Oberon pulled Syd across a landing to their room.

Once inside, Oberon wasted no time in pinning Syd against the closed door, capturing his lips in a searing kiss. He shrugged out of his sling. "Can't get close enough to you wearing this thing."

"Don't hurt yourself," Syd mumbled between kisses.

Oberon touched every part of Syd's body he could reach. They both shed their clothes in a frenzy of pulling and unbalanced hopping. The room was filled with the sound of their heavy breathing and the rustle of fabric hitting the floor. Naked, they crashed together in a passionate embrace. Oberon grabbed Syd's hair, holding him in place while he sucked up bruises on his neck.

"Jesus." Syd pressed his rock-hard erection into Oberon's hip.

They tumbled onto the bed in a tangle of limbs. Oberon extracted himself so he could trail kisses down Syd's body, exploring every crevice with his tongue. The chemistry between them was undeniable, a heady mix of lust and need. Adrenaline coursed through him, masking his aches and pains. "I'm going to make you mine again," Oberon said, his voice rough and low. He gripped Syd's dick and gave it a tug. "No pretence. No secrets."

Syd pushed into his hand. "Please!"

"But I think I should punish you first, don't you?" Oberon murmured. "For being a deceitful, lying, dishonest…"

"I get it! I'm sorry, okay? I'm in trouble with you for not telling you what I was up to and I'm in trouble with Uncle Mo for getting too attached. I can't win."

"What should I do to you, Sydenham?"

"Stop calling me that, for a start!"

"You didn't answer the question."

"Spanking. Spanking is good." Syd squirmed, clawing at the covers.

"Hmm, I don't think so. You'd enjoy it too much. I have a better idea."

"Oh…"

"You don't get to come."

"No!"

"Yes."

"What, not ever?"

"Don't give me those puppy eyes. They won't work. You get to come when I've forgiven you."

"Oh God. I'm too young to die."

"A bit of denial won't kill you. Suck it up, sunshine. In fact, you can start your penance by sucking it up. I'll be rating your blow-job skills."

Oberon sprawled on his back, legs spread. "Get to it."

"Well, if you insist." Syd smacked his lips together.

"I'm waiting, Syd." Oberon fisted his straining cock. "Best blow job ever. Now."

Syd reached for Oberon's shaft, his fingers trembling.

"Are you nervous, or do you not take orders well?" Oberon teased.

"Hey, there's a lot riding on this! Forgive me for feeling the pressure." Gently, Syd began stroking. His lips parted.

Oberon watched him intently and finally Syd wrapped his lips around the head of Oberon's cock. He swirled his tongue around it and sucked. Oberon closed his eyes, enjoying the warmth of Syd's mouth and his skilled tongue but then something changed. Syd's technique got more confident and he took Oberon deep, swallowing hard. Oberon held back a gasp and opened his eyes. Syd picked up the pace, working his lips harder, his eyes locked with Oberon's. The pleasure built, and Oberon started to slip towards the edge. He grabbed Syd's hair, forcing him to pause and pull away. "Not yet," he said, roughly releasing Syd's hair and leaning back into the pillows.

Syd reached for Oberon's cock again. He teased and seduced with tongue and teeth but never moved too fast. He seemed to be paying close attention to Oberon's reactions, adjusting his technique to please and frustrate. Oberon reached out and cupped Syd's neck, guiding his movements and urging him on. Syd was drawing him closer and closer to the edge. Waves of pleasure built inside him, the dizzying sensation of an impending orgasm just beyond his reach. He was nearing his limit. Syd worked his magic, coaxing him towards release. Finally, with his self-control in shreds, Oberon couldn't hold back any longer. He gripped the sheets tightly, his breath catching in his throat. With a hoarse cry, he came into Syd's mouth, holding him in place while he swallowed again and again.

Oberon collapsed back against the pillows, spent and sated. Syd licked his lips.

"Yum."

"That was…spectacular," Oberon admitted.

"I'm so hard it hurts."

"Good."

"You're a mean, evil man." Syd flopped down next to him, erection bobbing.

"I'm just getting started." Oberon grasped Syd's erection, stroking it slowly and deliberately. Syd moaned, his head falling back in pleasure, his hips bucking against Oberon's touch. Oberon leaned in closer to Syd, whose breaths were now coming in short, ragged gasps. He gently traced his fingers along Syd's chest, enjoying his shiver. "You want to come real bad, don't you?"

Syd's breath hitched. "Yes! I mean, yes please."

Oberon smirked and continued his sensual assault. He sought Syd's hole with the tip of a finger, eliciting a pleading sob. "More!" Syd's moans grew more insistent. He grabbed Oberon's wrist, trying to push his fingers deeper. "Please! I can't take much more."

Ignoring Syd's pleas, Oberon pulled his hand free, leaving Syd panting in frustration. Oberon chuckled, watching Syd squirm. "Ask me nicely."

"Damn it! Please, Oberon. I need it so much."

Oberon climbed on top of Syd and began to rub the head of his freshly erect dick against Syd's entrance.

"How are you hard again already?" Syd moaned.

"You're inspiring."

Syd writhed beneath him.

"I can keep this up for a long time. Tell me why you deserve to come."

Syd panted, his eyes locked on Oberon's. "I need it, Oberon. I've been thinking about it all day." He whimpered. "I want to feel you inside me, filling me up."

"And you're not ever going to lie to me again, are you?"

"No, never! I promise."

Oberon flicked the tip of Syd's cock. "And this is mine."

Syd nodded frantically, his eyes wide and pleading. "All yours."

"Then you'd best find me a condom, hadn't you?"

"Fuck!" Syd scrambled from beneath Oberon, half fell onto the floor then rummaged through his bag. "Yes!" He tossed the foil package and a bottle of lube to Oberon before diving back onto the bed. "Quick!"

Oberon tore open the package then rolled the condom onto his erect cock. The lube was slick and cold even through the rubber. "They need to make this stuff warmer!" He positioned himself at Syd's entrance, slowly pressing the head of his cock against it.

"Finally!" Syd muttered. "In me."

"Bossy brat." Oberon thrust forward, sinking into Syd with one powerful motion. Syd cried out, arching his back. Oberon grabbed Syd's legs, propping them on his shoulders so he could get closer.

"Your shoulder!" Syd protested.

"Painkillers are miraculous things, Syd." Oberon withdrew slightly, then thrust back in with rough force. Syd panted beneath him, his hips bucking to meet each of Oberon's thrusts.

"You want this, don't you?" Oberon growled. "You like it rough."

"Yes!" Syd cried, his voice hoarse. "Harder!"

Oberon obliged, increasing the pace and intensity of his thrusts. He tightened his grip on Syd's hips, his rhythm becoming more erratic as his second orgasm loomed.

Syd reached for the headboard, grabbing the rails. He clenched his inner muscles around Oberon's thrusts. "Oh, fuck!" Syd gasped, his voice strained. "I'm gonna come! Don't stop!"

Oberon thrust deeper and faster, matching Syd's desperation. He leaned forward, nipping at Syd's neck and ear. "I should put you in chastity. Lock that pretty cock in a cage. Keep you wanting."

With a loud cry, Syd came hard, his body shaking beneath Oberon. Oberon surged forward, emptying himself inside Syd's warm, tight heat. They stayed like that for a moment, locked together, both gasping for breath.

Finally, Oberon pulled out. He lowered Syd's legs to the bed then lay next to him, smiling. Syd stretched out, limp and spent, his face flushed and glistening with sweat. With a contented sigh, he turned to face Oberon.

"You're a devil, you know that?"

Oberon chuckled, even as he traced his fingertips lazily over Syd's damp skin. "I try my best," he said. "You enjoyed it."

"Hard not to," Syd admitted. "Did you mean that about putting me in chastity?"

"Something for you to wonder about."

"That's kind of terrifying. And exhilarating."

"Have we discovered a new kink?" Oberon asked.

"No! I mean...I don't think I want to be that powerless."

"Don't you? It's more about trust than power."

Syd shivered. "I get it. I do. I've given you no cause to trust me but I trust you. You *can* trust me, Obi. I promise. No more deception."

"Then we can explore together, can't we?"

"I'd like that."

Oberon gave Syd a long, slow kiss. "So would I. Very much."

Chapter Eleven

The following day, after breakfast, Oberon sat on the hotel terrace admiring the view. Syd arrived with two cups of coffee. He handed one over before taking a seat.

"Lifesaver. Thank you. This is a beautiful spot," Oberon said. He sipped his coffee with a contented sigh.

"We're lucky it's a clear day. Uncle Mo brought me here once when I was a kid. I think it was his birthday. We had an amazing Sunday lunch and played croquet on the lawn, would you believe. I always wanted to come back here. He cheats by the way, and not just at croquet."

"Good to know. Which lake is that? It doesn't look that far away."

"Buttermere. We can take a drive over there later if you want to. There's a footpath that goes right the way around it. You can walk from here but it might be a bit far for you at the moment."

"Some exercise would be good."

"How's your shoulder?"

"Not bad, actually. I'm going to use the sling for now because it aches but try to leave it off every so often. I don't want to look like an invalid."

"Are you okay? Only you sound a bit, I don't know, jaded."

"To be honest, I feel a bit odd. I mean, I'm glad not to be chasing all over the countryside and relieved I'm not a wanted man anymore, but I still feel tense. Like we should be doing something. I guess I want to know what's happening with Kairos Doukas."

"Enforced rest is never the most relaxing, is it?" Syd sipped his coffee.

"I feel restless, not rested. Don't you get the sense that something really big is about to happen?"

"Yes, I do, but we have to let the security services do their job. And now I sound like Uncle Mo. Damn."

Oberon chuckled. "You have a way to go yet. But the security services, that's you, isn't it? You're stuck here with me when you could be doing something a lot more exciting."

"I don't feel stuck. I'd much rather be here with you than in London and that's not me buttering you up. Watching you is important work too, and you're very easy on my eyes."

"If that's not buttering, I don't know what is."

Syd shrugged and for a while they sat in companionable silence. Then Oberon, still staring at the shimmering lake, said, "Do you not think it's possible that the situation with Doukas could be a distraction? I don't mean that it's fake, just that something else we're not seeing could be going on at the same time?"

"What makes you think that?" Syd asked.

"The Black Stone people went to a lot of trouble to track me to Scotland. They had to be very worried about what information Art Carew passed on to me and there are references in his notebook that don't seem to be linked to Doukas at all."

"We could take another look but Uncle Mo took the book with him, didn't he?"

"I might have copied down a few things…" Oberon admitted.

Syd stared at him. "You'd make a good spy."

"Not sure I'd be into all the skullduggery. I'm not a great liar."

"Ouch. On that uncomfortable note, I'll go fetch your…what is it, another notebook?"

"Some pages torn out of one. They're folded in the inside pocket of the jacket I was wearing yesterday."

While he waited for Syd to return, Oberon couldn't help but wonder what Mo was up to. He pictured him in a dimly lit office in some anonymous building in Whitehall, hatching plans with people who didn't use their real names. Somewhere even darker their enemies would be working on their own plans. He couldn't shake the feeling of danger and impending disaster, nor that he and Syd might be the ones best placed to deal with whatever was coming.

Syd returned and Oberon couldn't help but smile. "I didn't mean to make you feel bad. I'm sorry." He reached for Syd's hand. His fingers were cool. Syd leaned in for a kiss.

"And I shouldn't take offense so easily. I lie for a living, I *should* be good at it. I can't expect you to forgive *and* forget in a day."

"Forgive, yes, because there isn't anything *to* forgive. Forget…I have a long memory and intend to *milk* the situation for as long as possible. There are so many creative ways to punish naughty young spies."

"Giving you time alone to think is *way* too dangerous." Syd sat down. "I refuse to contemplate the alternative meanings of milking. So how about these notes?"

Oberon unfolded the pages. "I jotted down some of the things that Art repeated the most. Thirty-nine steps. Then later on he wrote *'thirty-nine steps – I counted them – high tide, 10.17 p.m.'* It has to be a clue."

"Art knew about Black Stone. He knew the people involved. Perhaps he also learned how they intended to leave the country after Doukas's death."

"So, it'll be tomorrow. Some place where high tide is at ten-seventeen in the evening," Syd said.

"What if they've already gone?" Oberon took his arm out of its sling and rested it on the chair arm. "That doesn't feel too bad."

"Be careful. You don't want to open the wound."

"Yes, Mom."

"I *will* get Fran on the phone to yell at you if you don't behave."

"An effective threat. I promise to take care."

Syd looked dubious. "Anyway, I think these people will stay in the country long enough to ensure their plan has been carried out. They'll want to celebrate and gloat."

"So we need the tides tables."

"If we go inside, I can look them up on the laptop. It'll be easier than peering at a phone screen."

The hotel had a small sitting room for guests with comfy chairs, bookcases and a cupboard full of board games. It was empty, so after Syd fetched his computer, they took possession of the table and closed the door.

After tapping away for a couple of minutes, Syd frowned. "There are hundreds of entries, it'll take forever to sort through them all. We need to narrow the search somehow."

"What did Art mean by steps?" Oberon said. "If he meant dock steps, why would he mention a specific number? It has to be some place where there are several staircases, and one of them has thirty-nine steps."

"Possibly. What about ferry sailings for the continent?" Syd searched but came up blank. "There's nothing that leaves at that time."

"Why is high tide so important? If it's a harbour, it must be a small one. I doubt they'd use a big boat from a popular port. So it must be some out of the way place where the tide is important, or perhaps where there's no harbour at all." Oberon knuckled his temples. "This is so frustrating."

"If it's a small place, what do the steps signify?" Syd asked. "We're going 'round in circles. My brain hurts."

"It's a puzzle. If only Art hadn't been so obtuse." Oberon sighed. "The man gave his life for this, we should be thankful we have anything to go on at all. He was worried about me knowing too much, but that was when he thought he would be dealing with it all himself."

"Let's think about it from a different angle," Syd suggested. "If you were someone wanting to get out of the country in secret, where would you leave from?"

"Not from any of the big harbours and not from the Channel coast or any of the obvious routes from the north-east towards Norway. There's too much surveillance, particularly where migrants might be trying to cross in small boats."

"So that leaves the west coast or Scotland."

"Probably not Scotland — there are submarine bases up there, lots of island ferries, fishing fleets…"

Syd tapped on his keyboard, bringing up a map of the west coast. "The tide times are wrong for Cornwall and Wales. Looks like here in Cumbria is the most likely."

"So, what do we think we know?" Oberon sat forward in his chair. "We're looking for a place with several sets of stairs, one with thirty-nine steps. High tide is at ten-seventeen p.m. and it's only possible to leave the shore at that time."

Syd zoomed in on the Cumbrian cost. "Not a harbour then, open coast. I think we're looking at a fishing trawler or maybe a yacht. A vessel that can anchor off shore, but not so far that a small boat couldn't reach it."

"I wonder if there's an Ordnance Survey map in here somewhere." Oberon got to his feet with a groan. "Fuck, everything hurts."

"That's what happens when you blow yourself up," Syd said, straight faced.

"I did not explode myself…okay, I guess I did…but there's no need to remind me."

"You also had a car accident *and* took a header off a bike."

Oberon glared at him. "Yes. Thanks. I am aware." He limped over to the bookshelves. He found a stack of local maps and pulled out the ones that covered the coastline. "Score!" He spread one out on the table then pored over it while Syd continued to search on the computer.

"Fuck me!" Oberon exclaimed a few minutes later.

"Is that an invitation?" Syd asked. "Because I'd rather it was the other way round to be honest. Though you do have an exceptional ass."

"No, you idiot. Look at this." Oberon stabbed at the map with a finger. "I think I've got it."

Syd stood then circled the table. "Show me."

"There." Oberon couldn't believe what he'd found.

"Fuck me."

"Exactly!"

"St. Eps Manor. It's practically on the beach." Syd went back to his computer. "St. Eps is short for Saint Ephrem. Ephrem is the patron saint for spiritual directors and spiritual leaders. According to this, he 'took upon himself the special task of opposing the many false doctrines rampant at his time, always remaining a true and forceful defender of the Catholic Church'. Interesting."

"Surely that has to be the place we're looking for," Oberon said. "It can't be a coincidence, but the only cliffs on this coastline are at St Bees and this is further south. It's unlikely to have thirty-nine steps onto the beach. Please don't let it be another dead end."

"But now we know it was St. Eps, not steps, so perhaps the thirty-nine is something different too," Syd suggested.

"Of course. So what's significant about the number thirty-nine?"

"Let me see what Wikipedia has to say. Source of all random knowledge. Okay, so among other things, thirty-nine in religion doesn't seem to include anything useful unless you're interested in the number of mentions of work or labour in the Torah."

"Uh, no. I don't think that's it."

"It's the title of a song by the Cure on their album *Bloodflowers*."

"Good band, but probably not."

"It's the traditional number of times citizens of Ancient Rome hit their slaves when beating them, referred to as 'forty save one'. Wow, you learn something new every day."

"All very interesting, but..." Oberon was getting frustrated. "It's a bit of a stretch."

"Oh, fuck." Syd paled.

"What?"

"It was the duration, in nanoseconds, of the nuclear reaction in the largest nuclear explosion ever performed."

"Why is that significant?" Oberon wasn't sure he wanted to know the answer.

"Because Sellafield, Europe's largest nuclear site, is also on this part of the coast and I don't believe in coincidences. Sellafield has the most diverse range of nuclear facilities in the world on a single site. It doesn't generate power anymore but it does process nuclear waste, stores it, and conducts nuclear decommissioning."

"So blowing it up would cause a global incident." Oberon sat down.

"It would also serve to destroy any chance of nuclear power being seen as a safe energy option compared to fossil fuels and could start World War Three if certain countries could be blamed."

Oberon put his head in his hands. "This is a nightmare."

"Nazi Germany invaded Poland and kicked off World War Two in 1939."

"Double, triple fuck." Oberon looked at Syd, who was chewing a fingernail. "I think you should call your godfather, don't you?"

"Yeah. Fuck, Obi, I hope we're wrong." Syd looked at his mobile then froze.

"What is it?"

"News alert on the BBC. Kairos Doukas was shot and killed half an hour ago."

Oberon stared at Syd. "How can that be possible? Damn it! I though Mo was going to keep him safe."

"So did I," Syd said. "Let's not jump to conclusions. Let me call him and find out what the heck is going on."

Chapter Twelve

It took a while for Syd to be put through to Mo because of the number of gatekeepers protecting him from unwanted calls. "No secrets. Full disclosure, Uncle Mo isn't usually my boss," Syd said. "He's way above my pay grade at work. He roped me into stalking you as a favour."

"Not sure whether I should thank him or demand compensation," Oberon said.

"Hey!"

Oberon chuckled. "Okay, I'll take your exceptionally cute behind as reparation."

"Sadly, I don't think there's going to be any taking for a while." Syd eventually got to Mo's personal assistant who knew Syd and had the sense to connect him. Syd put the phone on loudspeaker on the table between him and Oberon. Mo finally picked up the call.

"I wondered how long it would take you to call me, Syd. You never could do as you're told, though as it happens I was about to call *you*."

"We saw the news about Doukas. What happened?"

"You shouldn't believe everything you see on the news, Sydenham, especially in this deep fake age. You don't need to worry about Doukas. He's fine. Winded but nothing more thanks to a bullet-proof vest and now safely stashed away at great cost to the taxpayer."

"It looked so real. Your level of sneaky far outstrips mine, Uncle Mo."

"I'm flattered. I think."

Oberon pictured Mo shaking his head. "Tell him the rest, Syd."

"Is that Oberon with you? Did you two try communicating with each other?"

"I don't think my relationship issues should be the topic of the moment," Syd said. "But yes. We did." He leered at Oberon. "But I need to tell you what we've worked out." Syd recounted everything they'd deciphered and their fear that Sellafield might be a target. When he'd finished there's was a moment's silence.

"Listen to me carefully, both of you," Mo said. "As farfetched as it all seems, we've had intelligence from a different source that confirms your suspicions."

"Holy fuck," Syd muttered.

"Quite. Now, if you could listen for more than five seconds…"

"Sorry."

"We believe that an attack will come from the sea. Several Soviet medium-range ballistic missiles are known to have been sold on the black market recently and the warning nets in the Atlantic have picked up some interesting traffic in recent days."

"What the hell can we do about that?" Syd said.

"It's not for you to worry about. The Royal Navy enjoys a challenge and our American friends are always up for a party."

"How are you this calm and collected?" Oberon butted in.

"My dear boy, there's little point in getting in a flap now, is there? Cool heads will prevail. However, we do need to gain the boat boys and girls some time."

"Why do I get the feeling I'm not going to like what you're about to say?" Syd ran a hand through his hair, making it stand up in tufts.

"Ah, well. Here's where you get to earn your salary."

"Oh God."

"We think that Oberon's Black Stone acquaintances will have been waiting for confirmation of Doukas's shooting. That will be their queue to leave the country in advance of ordering the missile attack. I want you to delay them, Syd."

"You want me to...that's making one hell of an assumption that we're right and that they'll be at St. Ephrem's Manor."

"Oh, it's not an assumption. They are."

"And just how do you know that?" Syd glared at the phone as if Mo could see his expression. Oberon couldn't help but smile.

"After Oberon's adventures in Scotland, I've had people looking into the owner of the house he blew up."

"It was only a small explosion," Oberon muttered.

"Quite. Well, the owner of that, now rather charred property also owns..."

"The Manor," Syd interjected. "And that would be Dougal McLeish, I assume."

"Indeed. A nasty piece of work with some very dubious associates. It stands to reason that his friends would head there. Their escape was probably planned round it, in fact. Art Carew's notes confirm that the manor is their departure point."

"So what do you want me to do?" Syd asked.

"Slow them down. The longer it is before they leave, the longer we have to find the missile launch craft and stop the attack. The Atlantic is not a fish pond, you know. The search has to be narrowed carefully."

"Is that all." Syd pursed his lips. "Are you going to send someone else to keep an eye on Oberon?"

Oberon grabbed the phone. "Give us a moment, Morris." He put it on mute. "If you think for one second you're leaving me here while you go looking for these people alone, you're very much mistaken."

"I..."

"No. Not going to happen."

"This is my job, Obi. It's not yours."

"Who fucking cares? Art trusted me with this. I owe him. And besides, I'd prefer you keep breathing. I need to be around to make sure that happens."

Syd's pained sigh spoke volumes but he picked up the phone. "Okay. We'll do what we can." He listened, wincing. "Do you think I don't know that? He's more stubborn than Fran. Yes, she's scarier...where's this going? Fine, I'll try to make sure he doesn't get any more broken than he already is." He disconnected the call. "You're gonna get me fired."

Oberon shrugged. "Ow. Shouldn't have done that."

"Oh my God."

"Don't start thinking you're in charge, sunshine."

"I *am* in charge!"

"I'll let you think you are for a while. So, what's the plan?"

Syd's expression was one of stubborn frustration. "I can't believe Mo said yes to this."

"Probably realized we come as a package deal. He's a clever man."

"God helps us all. Fine. Let's go birdwatching."

"I...don't know what to do with that." Oberon had been considering lots of options. That wasn't one of them.

"Think about it, it's the perfect cover. Binoculars, on the beach at dusk, we can take snacks." Syd grinned.

"You're cracked." Oberon thought about it. "It could work."

"Of course it could. We need to get close and keep an eye on them. We only need to intervene if they try to get to sea somehow. Just up the coast at St. Bees, the cliffs are home to all sorts of seabirds. It won't be out of the ordinary for birdwatchers to be out and about and because the tide isn't high until after dark, we should have time to get into a good position."

"It's so daft, it might work."

"Who are you calling daft?"

"If the shoe fits."

"Hmm. This discussion isn't over but I need to get a few things together."

While Syd gathered their outdoor gear, Oberon borrowed some binoculars from the receptionist along with a dog-eared copy of the *Collins Guide to British Birds*. They met outside by the car.

"Ready?" Oberon asked.

"I'm not exactly equipped with spy stuff here," Syd said. "We'll have to make the best of it." He stuffed his small pack onto the back seat. Oberon added his birding accessories then they set off, with Syd driving. The route to the coast meandered through pretty winding lanes edged by looming fells. The weather wasn't too bad but the hills cast long, dark shadows.

"I'm not sure I could live here all year round," Oberon commented. "I imagine it can be bleak in winter."

"It's beautiful but I feel the same," Syd agreed. "I'd love a holiday place here. Somewhere quiet like Uncle Mo has, but not too overshadowed by the fells."

"Even though you can escape to Scotland whenever you want?"

"Scotland has a lot of responsibilities attached to it," Syd said. "If I'm there at the same time as my parents, my dad wants to teach me all about estate management. I keep trying to tell him that Fran is far more suited to that life than I am but he hasn't given up yet."

"Your dad not feeling your career choices?"

"Which considering they chose my godfather is entirely on them." Syd laughed. "If it wasn't for a childhood full of Uncle Mo's spy games, I wouldn't have been enticed into the service."

"Does it cause friction?"

"They don't mind really. They think I have a steady office job and want the bright lights of London. I'll bring them round. I can't do anything about the title but I can make sure Fran gets the estate."

"So London's home?"

"For now. And you'll have to come visit. I have a place in Belgravia...another shameful advantage of family money and property."

"I'm not judging."

"No, you're not, are you? A lot of people only see pound signs."

"Difficult to make good friends you can trust, then."

"Tell me about it."

"Do you need to work at all, Syd?"

"For the money? No. For my sanity? Yes."

"Your sanity...there's a topic for further discussion." Oberon snorted with laughter.

"Hey! Your status there is nothing to shout about."

"Probably why we're so well suited."

Syd blushed. "We are, aren't we?"

"This is getting a little too close to sharing our feelings," Oberon said.

"Good point. We are clearly failures as men. Anyway, we're here, so no need for any more oversharing." Syd turned the car into a National Trust car park, beaming from ear to ear.

"Idiot."

"Grouch." Syd hopped out of the car then grabbed his bag from the back. "I've got bottled water, snacks, a map and I can take your bird book."

Oberon slung the binoculars on a strap around his neck and pulled a woolly hat over his distinctive hair. They followed a rough path through the trees from the car park then strolled along the beach, which was backed by a scrub-covered slope. After a couple of false starts, Syd found a good observation point.

"There's a clear view from here," Oberon said. "I can see the manor." With the binoculars he could make out the house in detail. "I see landscaping, a tennis court, and flagpole with a Union Jack up it."

"Ironic, considering what they're up to," Syd muttered. "They probably see themselves as patriots."

"No doubt. Fucking extremists. There's a raised area in front of the house with steps down to the gardens. Looks like there's gated access to the beach." Oberon leaned against a grassy hummock, making himself comfortable. "It's the ideal spot for an escape by sea. Convenient that they hooked up with your Scottish neighbour."

"They would have done their research and targeted him deliberately. Made him think he was important. He has an ego the size of a planet."

"I hope Mo is after him too."

"No doubt. You take first watch," Syd said. "We'll swap in half an hour so you can rest your eyes. It's hard work staring through those things. In the meantime, I'll test the snacks for quality."

A few minutes before they were due to change over, Oberon spotted someone leave the house and saunter along the terrace in front of it. "Syd, someone's come out. I see a man, white trousers, blue jacket, and a hat. He's carrying binoculars and a newspaper. Okay, he's sitting on a bench on the terrace and using the glasses to look out to sea." Oberon watched while the man alternated between reading his paper and viewing the horizon. After twenty minutes he got up and went back into the house. "He's gone in." Oberon handed his binoculars to Syd. "Your turn."

Syd took over. "They must be waiting for a boat. Did you recognise him?"

Oberon shook his head. "He *could* be the old guy from the house in Scotland, Frobisher, but I'm not certain. Frobisher was bald, this guy had a hat on. He didn't move like a young man though, so it's possible. He didn't give any indication that he knew he was being watched, so that's good."

"Too arrogant to believe anyone's onto them." Syd turned his line of sight out to sea. "Hmm. Three hours till high tide and at this time of year it'll only just be getting dark by then. I think their transport has arrived." Syd pointed to the west.

Oberon squinted at the horizon. "Nice."

"Some billionaire's super yacht no doubt. It's flying Bermuda's colours. Name is…" Syd adjusted the binoculars.

"Ariadne," said Oberon with certainty.

"How did you know?"

"Art's notebook. It was one of the names he mentioned. It was an oddity because most of the other names were surnames."

"Fuck me."

"Later."

"Pinky swear?"

"If I must." Oberon held out a finger and Syd squeezed it.

"They're going to need a way to get to the yacht. It'll get a bit closer at high tide but they'll still need to send a tender in to the beach."

Oberon massaged his shoulder, easing some of the ache. "If they knew that Art had discovered this part of their plan, they'd have changed location, wouldn't they?"

"Or not worried that one man would be believed by the authorities. Killing Art was a precaution, hunting you down was likely the same." Syd rummaged in his pack and extracted a chocolate bar. "Want some?"

Oberon shook his head. "No thanks." He stared at the house. "I think I might have a way of delaying them though."

Syd gave him a speculative look as he munched his chocolate. "I suspect this idea is going to suck. Big time. Why is that?"

"Intuition?"

"Okay, spill it. What's going round that head of yours?"

Oberon wrapped his arms around his knees. "I'm a loose end for Black Stone, aren't I? Finding out how much I know, if I can identify them, if I have the notebook...they might believe their plan to kill Kairos Doukas succeeded but if your godfather is right and they plan to destroy a nuclear site...that'll make them wanted men the world over. There won't be many places to run."

"So...?"

"I could get closer to the house. Make sure I'm seen. They'll think I'm picking up where Art left off."

"I knew it. That's the worst plan I've ever heard."

"Yeah, possibly, but do you have any better ideas? All Mo needs us to do is buy time. Every minute could make a difference, couldn't it?"

Syd rolled onto his side. He propped his chin in one hand. "I can't decide if you're brave or dumber than a box of those rocks you dig out of the ground."

"I'm no hero so it must be the latter." Oberon cupped Syd's cheek. "Stopping these people is far more important than you or me. Preventing another world war is kind of imperative, don't you think?"

"What's a planet or two between friends?" Syd frowned. "I'm not going to stop you, am I?"

"No." Oberon's breath came out in a whoosh as Syd flattened him before peppering his face with kisses.

"Trust me to fall for a dumbass."

"Are you crying?" Oberon pulled away. He followed the damp trail of a tear on Syd's cheek with his thumb.

"No, of course not. It's the sea air."

"Right." A long, lingering kiss followed. "You mustn't be worrying about me because you'll have your own job to do."

"Which is?"

"While I slow them down in the house, you'll have to handle the beach. You have to stop the tender coming in."

Syd's eyes glinted. "I can do that. I'll need an hour."

"I can keep them busy that long. What are you going to do?"

"You'll see, but for now its best you don't know. We need them to think you're alone. You'd better take the pack so it appears as if you were in for the long haul watching them."

"Okay. I'd better not hang around. They could be planning to leave any moment." Oberon got to his feet, ignoring the various aches and pains of bruises and cuts. "Be careful, Syd."

"Me?" Syd shook his head. "You're the one walking into the lion's den."

"Even so. They could have observers watching the beach that we don't know about. The people coming in from the yacht could have weapons…"

"All right, I promise I'll take care."

After another sensuous kiss they separated. Oberon circled back and made his way down the beach towards the sea. The tide was creeping in and he walked just ahead of the tideline along the next stretch of sand. He made a pretence of using the binoculars before turning towards the manor. He reached the gate that provided access to the beach from the property without incident and crouched low by the fence. The gardens followed a gentle incline, which allowed him a decent view of the terrace and it wasn't long before the man he'd seen before appeared again. This time he'd forgone the hat and Oberon could be sure that it was the same older man who had threatened him in Scotland—Selwyn Frobisher, with the cold, hooded eyes.

His heart raced as he watched Frobisher on the terrace through the binoculars. Memories of being hunted across the moors, being trapped and the explosion flooded his mind. Frobisher was speaking into a mobile, the sound of his voice carried by the wind but too faint for Oberon to make out any words. He seemed agitated, his hand gestures and pacing suggesting anger. "Something's put the wind up him," Oberon muttered. "Good."

Suddenly, Frobisher turned and scanned the beach below. Oberon's breath caught and he prayed he hadn't been spotted. Discovery needed to be on his terms. After a moment that felt like an eternity, Frobisher shrugged then returned to his call. Oberon took out his mobile and snapped a few pictures, zooming in as far as he could. He sent the clearest one to Syd and was about to take more when a sudden noise made him freeze. Glancing over his shoulder, Oberon saw two men emerging from the scrub.

Damn. He scrambled to his feet and made a run for it. Though he wanted to get caught, he had to make it look like he was desperate to get away. The men behind him shouted something he couldn't hear over the wind and waves. They gained on him quickly. He recognized them as the other two men from Scotland, one big and bulky, moving clumsily through the sand, the other dark and lean. Looking back was his undoing. He tripped and crashed to the ground, holding back a scream as his battered body made contact with unforgiving, hard-packed sand. Winded, he gasped for air. He attempted to get to his feet but then there was a knee in his back, his arms were yanked behind him and he was hauled to his feet.

It was late in the evening and other than a solitary dog walker some distance away, there was no one around. Oberon doubted Syd could see what was happening because the terrain was full of hidden dips. Great for sheltering picnickers from the wind, they weren't so good for maintaining a line of sight. *It doesn't matter. Syd has things he needs to be getting on with. This was my bright idea – I just hope I haven't bitten off more than I can chew.*

Oberon struggled enough to make it seem like he was trying to pull free. The big guy holding him grunted at the effort until his smaller colleague pulled a knife. He pressed it to Oberon's side.

"Unless you want me to fillet you like a salmon, keep still and come with us quietly."

The blade was sizeable with a wicked, serrated curve. There was enough menace in the man's voice to convince Oberon that his words weren't an empty threat. He decided he'd prefer not to find out how the knife felt slipping between his ribs. *Hickman, that's his name. The big guy is Rownham. I remember.*

"Where are we going?" A rough shove to the shoulder sent him stumbling in the direction of the manor.

"Someone wants a word."

After that, neither of the men said anything more. They herded Oberon across the sand to the gate at the bottom of the manor's grounds, then through it into the gardens. Oberon moved as slowly as he could get away with. In the fading light, the house loomed over them. It had a forbidding air, not helped by the dark green-grey of Lakeland slate walls.

They crunched across the gravelled terrace before Oberon was pushed into the house through a set of patio doors. They'd gone into what seemed to be a formal sitting room afflicted by a preponderance of floral chintz. It led on to a central hallway decked out to resemble a baronial manor. Dark oak panelling made it gloomy and the subjects of the oil paintings on the walls were uniformly unhappy, even the animals.

The guy that owns his place has delusions of grandeur. Oberon glanced around. *Figures. Stuffed animals in glass boxes give me the creeps.* Oberon's random thoughts were interrupted when they were joined by Selwyn Frobisher. A restraining hand on Oberon's arm prevented him from moving.

"Good evening, Mr. Wycherley. How nice we should meet again so soon." Frobisher's eyes gleamed.

"The pleasure is all yours," Oberon muttered. It wasn't difficult to relate these men to Art's brutal murder or to maniacal plans for the destruction of world peace. *Maybe one of them will try an evil cackle soon.*

"Now, now. Humility in defeat please. We are all gentlemen here."

Fuck me, this idiot is insane. "Just the three of you here to take over the world then?" Oberon knew he was pushing his luck, but he didn't have much to lose.

"Three here. Many others of like mind around the world, I can assure you." Frobisher circled him. I was disappointed that you chose to reject my hospitality in Scotland. Still, we have much to discuss and this time I won't be so careless as to leave you in a room full of explosives."

"I don't know what you want from me."

"Oh, I think you do. Search him."

Rownham, who Oberon could now see had scorched hair on one side of his head, searched Oberon roughly. He emptied his pack onto the floor, grunting at the innocuous contents. Spotting Oberon's mobile, he ground his heel into it. Splinters of glass shot across the floor. Oberon gritted his teeth against the pain as his jacket was yanked off.

"What do you expect to find? I was out doing a spot of birdwatching, that's all."

"Credit me with a modicum of intelligence," Frobisher spat, getting far too close for comfort. "Who are you working with?" His breath was hot on Oberon's neck.

"He was alone when we found him. We didn't have time to go searching for the other one," Hickman said, polishing the blade of his knife on his coat sleeve.

Fear clawed at Oberon's chest as he realized they had to be talking about Syd. *How did they spot us? I have to warn him somehow.* The chances of that were slim to none. Before Oberon could even consider his options, a sharp blow to his temple sent colours exploding behind his eyes then everything went dark.

Chapter Thirteen

Regaining consciousness wasn't a happy experience. Every part of Oberon's body had hurt *before* he'd been knocked out, now he had another pounding headache to add to his misery. *I'm going to need a brain scan with the number of times I've bashed my skull over the last two weeks. Fuck, I'd kill for an aspirin.* His head was hanging forward, so he lifted it, neck muscles protesting. It took his brain a few more seconds to register that he was bound to a chair and gagged with something that dug into the corners of his mouth. The metallic taste of blood coated his tongue. He tested the bonds holding him to a sturdy wooden chair but the thick black tape didn't budge. With a huff of exasperation he focused on his surroundings instead. He'd been moved but the room had to be in the manor. The dim light filtering through diamond-paned windows revealed a bare wooden floor and dusty furniture. There were golf-clubs and tennis-rackets leaning against a wall. A Victorian hat stand held straw hats and caps, a collection of walking sticks and umbrellas. A stack of neatly folded coats and waterproofs covered the top of an old oak chest, there was a grandfather clock ticking and some polished brass warming-pans on the walls. Wellington boots sat in a haphazard pile, emitting a musty smell that made Oberon's head swim. *It's a boot room, probably in the basement. Just one small window...* He twisted as far as he could and spotted a door in one corner standing ajar. Beyond it a stone staircase rose into darkness. *Where are they?* He yanked at his taped wrists but succeeded only in ripping some hair out. The chair was solid and too heavy to tip. He was worried about Syd. Oberon wanted Frobisher's attention on him and nowhere else, so the sound of footsteps descending the stairs was a mixed blessing. He glared as Frobisher appeared in front of him, a cruel smile on his face. His two companions lurked at the side of the room.

Frobisher tapped a finger against his lips. He hooded his eyes slowly and it was that that Oberon recalled most clearly from Scotland. It was a small thing, lasting only a second, but distinctive. Somewhere in the house, a clock struck ten. The urgency of the hour clarified Oberon's thoughts. He would place money that it had been the slight, dark man, Hickman, who had murdered Art Carew. There was a ruthless fervour in his eyes. *Perhaps he was also the one to put a bullet in Kairos Doukas.* Rownham, the bigger man who had tackled Oberon on the beach, had less distinct features. *He could merge into a crowd. I wonder if he was the one who had first tracked Art, and left his card in the mailbox. He'd be a threatening presence lurking in the dark.*

Selwyn Frobisher was the worst of the bunch. The initial benevolence he had affected in Scotland was long gone. His eyes had the inhuman luminosity of a bird's. There was more reflected in those eyes than triumph. A white heat of fanaticism burned in them, and Oberon realized for the first time what he'd been up against. *This man will stop at nothing to get what he wants. He's the brains behind all of this, I'm sure of it.*

"Time for us to have that chat," Frobisher sneered, circling Oberon like a vulture eyeing its prey. "You're a troublemaker, Mr. Wycherley. Did you really think you could get the better of us? You're one unprepared man against an organisation that spans the globe."

Oberon glared at him, more defiant than he thought he'd be considering the circumstances and the knot of dread in his stomach. He had to buy Syd more time. He was relieved that the three men were in the room with him because it meant they hadn't found Syd. That gave him hope that they still stood a chance of preventing disaster.

Frobisher crouched in front of Oberon, the scent of expensive cologne making his nose itch. "You're going to tell me everything you know," he whispered, his voice cold and threatening. Oberon didn't attempt to talk around the gag. He clenched his jaw and stared back at Frobisher with unwavering determination not to show fear. Frobisher's smile widened, contrasting sharply with the malice in his eyes. "Very well," Frobisher said, straightening up. "Let's see how resilient our friend here truly is."

Rownham struck Oberon across the face, the force of the blow making his head snap to the side. Pain exploded behind Oberon's eyes, but he refused to cry out. He wouldn't give them the satisfaction.

The interrogation was brutal and relentless but Oberon remained steadfast in his silence, enduring blow after blow. After a while, Frobisher removed the gag but Oberon refused to utter a word. Frobisher grew more frustrated with every passing moment, his veneer of civility slipping to expose the toxic underbelly beneath.

As the sun finally gave up on the day and darkness enveloped the room, Oberon slumped forwards, his breath ragged and laboured. Frobisher leaned in close, his voice a venomous whisper against Oberon's ear.

"You think you can outlast us? You think you're playing some heroic game?" he sneered. "You have no idea what you've got yourself into. Do you *want* to die?"

Oberon raised his head slowly, meeting Frobisher's gaze. "Fuck. You."

In that moment, a hint of fear flickered across Frobisher's face before he concealed it with a cold mask of indifference. "Time to demonstrate your skills with a blade, Mr. Hickman. Start with a finger, then perhaps an eye…"

If he'd been expecting Oberon to blurt out everything he knew, Frobisher was wrong. Oberon *was* debating his options though. *Have I bought Syd enough time?*

Hickman was trying to force Oberon to open the fist he was clenching when the sound of shouting filtered into the room from outside. Frobisher cursed and ordered Rownham to find out what was happening.

Rownham lumbered out and returned in less than five minutes. "There's a fire on the beach. There are dozens of people down there. I think they're having a fucking rave."

Frobisher's eyes widened in disbelief at his colleague's words. "The boat…" He turned back to

Oberon, his features twisted in fury. "This isn't over," he hissed, before storming out of the room with Rownham and Hickman close behind him. The muffled sounds of chaos from outside filtered into the room, a cacophony of shouting and distant sirens. *Syd must have organized a riot!*

With a surge of adrenaline, Oberon worked on loosening his restraints, his fingers fumbling and clumsy in the dim light. After what felt like an eternity, he got one hand free. That made getting rid of the rest of the tape a lot easier but it still took time. He stood up unsteadily, his body protesting every movement from the beating he had endured. He couldn't afford to wait for Frobisher to return. Pushing through the dizziness, Oberon made his way to the door and cautiously opened it a crack. He climbed the stairs, wincing with every step. On the next floor, the hallway was empty, but he could still hear the faint sounds from outside echoing through the manor. He peered out of the first window he came to. There was a huge bonfire on the beach and he could make out dozens of figures against the orange light. "You don't mess about, do you, Syd?" He grinned even though it hurt his face.

Limping, he made his way through the house. He found the room he'd been brought in through and retraced his steps through the garden to the beach gate. He had to move slowly because every inch of him hurt but no one tried to stop him. He headed towards the lights and found a lively crowd of young people gathered around a huge fire worthy of November fifth, their faces illuminated by the dancing flames. The night air was brisk, and many were bundled in hoodies, beanies and scarves. Some sat on driftwood logs or blankets spread out on the sand, while others stood, clutching mugs of steaming drinks. Someone was playing a guitar. A few people were playing a raucous game of touch football. Oberon weaved between them, getting a few concerned looks.

A makeshift grill was set up nearby, sizzling with burgers and sausages, adding the scent of food to the salty sea breeze. Occasionally, someone threw another log onto the fire, sending a shower of sparks into the air and making the flames leap higher. Oberon caught orange reflections on the water as waves crashed into shore, adding to the noise.

Stumbling, he made his way through the crowd, hunting for Syd. He found him on the tideline, yelling into his phone. As soon as he spotted Oberon, Syd stopped talking then ran towards him. Oberon dropped to his knees in the sand, his relieved laughter tinged with hysteria.

"Look at the fucking state of you!" Syd muttered, reaching for Oberon's face. "You're covered in blood."

"It's nothing serious," Oberon slurred. "They hadn't progressed to the good stuff before your distraction did its thing. Have to say your timing was spot on. Any longer and I might have lost a few body parts. How did you manage all this?" Oberon gestured vaguely at the people around him.

"That can wait. I need to get you to a hospital."

"Don't need one. Really. I'm just a bit battered. What about the tender from the yacht, did it make it to shore?"

"Turned back when we lit the big bonfire," Syd said. He helped Oberon to his feet. "They weren't interested in joining the party, apparently."

"Where did all these people come from, Syd?"

"I have a lot of friends around here. I spent most summers here as a kid, remember? I mobilized anyone and everyone I could get hold of via social media, made a few calls, got the landlord of the local pub to set up the food…he dated Fran a while back so didn't dare say no. There are often impromptu parties on the beach and stacks of driftwood gets stashed in the dunes. The nightlife around here isn't so exciting that people had anything more interesting to do and once word got round…" He shrugged. "Friends come when you call."

"It was a genius move." Oberon limped to the edge of the water and stared out to sea. "What's going on out there?"

"About now, His Majesty's Coastguard is boarding the Ariadne," Syd said, bouncing gleefully. "One super yacht is about to be impounded."

"What about the men from the manor? It was the same bunch as in Scotland. The old guy with the cold eyes is Frobisher, the slight, dark haired one is Hickman and the big guy is Rownham. I sent you pictures of Frobisher."

"The pictures alongside the names will save Uncle Mo some time, I'm sure. I already sent him your snaps. The local police have been alerted so they'll be tracked down soon enough. Not sure what the sentence for treason is these days."

"And what about Sellafield, is it safe?"

"That's what I was on the phone about, trying to find out if the Navy has done its thing, but there wasn't any news."

"You were yelling."

"I was mad. I thought you'd sacrificed yourself for nothing but if missiles *were* launched, we'd be able to see the flames at Sellafield from here." As Syd spoke, there was a streak of light across the sky followed by an explosion. The roar of fighter jets passed close overhead. "Fuck! I think the flyboys just took out a missile!" Syd's expression was of wide-eyed horror.

Oberon drew him into a hug. "That couldn't have been any closer."

"I think it gave me a new hair parting and I may need clean underwear." Syd's phone beeped. He took a quick look then held it up so that Oberon could see the text message that had been delivered.

Mission accomplished. Mo.

They stared at each other. "So, it's over?" Oberon asked.

"It's over."

Water lapped over Oberon's boots but he didn't care. Syd's warmth soaked into him. "So what happens now?"

Syd shrugged. "I say we go back to the hotel and test the resilience of the bedsprings." He eyed Oberon. "Or maybe put you to bed with pain meds."

"You don't want to join in the fun?" Oberon turned to watch sparks flying from the bonfire. People were partying as if nothing had happened. "They don't seem to have noticed anything unusual."

"There are low flying jets across here all the time. There's beer and barbecue to be had. Priorities." Syd smiled. "The world goes on. None of them know what you've been through the last few weeks."

"What *we've* been through." Oberon swayed and Syd steadied him.

"I want to be with you," Syd murmured. "And you need to be in bed."

"You have a one-track mind."

Syd frowned. "I could have lost you, Obi. Don't ever do that to me again. What if they'd...?"

"It was a fair guess that they'd want information out of me first, and they did. I was lucky they had no chance to set up a proper torture chamber. It was more brute force and ignorance."

"Even so. I don't like the whole self-sacrificing hero bit. My nerves can't take it."

"I've no intention of getting into this kind of mess again. I must learn to appreciate the benefits of a boring life."

"Life with me is never boring, honeybun."

"Call me that again and I'll introduce you to my flogger collection, brat."

Syd beamed. "Sounds like a deal...*honeybun*. Let's go."

A sharp crack split the air and Oberon slumped. The pain followed. Burning agony that radiated from his shoulder until it consumed the rest of his body. His vision swam. He pressed a shaky hand to his collarbone and his fingers came away sticky with blood.

"Fuck. I don't think our Black Stone friends are too pleased that we've ruined their plans."

Syd lowered him to the ground. "You got shot, you idiot!" He ripped at Oberon's clothes, exposing the wound. "What did I just say to you? Were you listening at all? No. You're determined to give me heart failure."

"Hurts."

"No shit, genius. A hole in your body tends to do that." Syd's voice was edged with panic. He pressed a wadded handkerchief over the wound then groped for his mobile.

"You carry a proper cotton hanky."

"Doesn't everyone?" Syd made a frantic call for an ambulance. Once help was on the way, he knelt in the sand and put Oberon's head in his lap. "Don't you dare fucking die on me. I swear, I'll kill you myself."

"You're making no sense."

"Nothing new there then. Keep still. Talk to me. No sleeping."

"Where's the shooter, Syd? Shouldn't you take cover?"

"Not sure, it's dark. The party crowd has scattered and there's no sign anyone else was hurt. They targeted you. You really must have pissed them off."

"Tried my best. Bought you enough time."

"Okay, so one of them is running into the sea with two local coppers after him. Not sure what he thinks he's going to accomplish unless he intends to swim to Ireland."

"The old guy, Frobisher, is the really dangerous one. I'm sure he's behind all this."

"And I can see him walking back towards the manor. He's been stopped by the cops. He's probably saying something like 'don't you know who I am?' in a pompous voice."

Despite the pain, Oberon chuckled. Syd's running commentary on events was keeping him conscious, which now Oberon thought about it, was probably Syd's plan.

"There's another one."

"Yeah. Big guy. Just got tackled by a cop who must be playing rugby on the weekends. He's flattened him. Nice. And the ambulance is here. I can see more blue lights flashing on the beach road."

"Bit cold."

Syd took off his coat and laid it over Oberon. "I noticed that about you. You have a tendency to warm your feet up on me in bed."

"Do not!"

"Do so… Oberon? Hey…stay awake."

Syd's voice faded, merging with the sound of the waves. Oberon was aware of people in green looming over him. There were voices but no distinct words. He was tired and could no longer resist the urge to close his eyes. His last thought was that he'd had a decent innings and gone out on a high.

Epilogue

For north-west England, August was doing a decent impression of summer. It had been eight weeks since Oberon and Syd had saved the world, as Syd liked to describe it. Oberon felt that there were a few other people involved that deserved some credit and that their part had been small, but he'd given up arguing.

"It was good of your Uncle Mo to lend us the cottage," Oberon said, settling back in his sun lounger, glass of iced water in hand.

"He had an ulterior motive," Syd grumbled.

"He offered me a job, sweetheart. Doesn't mean I have to take it."

"You need a longer break. Two weeks in hospital, six weeks recuperation…I want you to myself for at least another month."

"Your leave of absence isn't indefinite. You'll have to go back sooner or later."

Syd put his unread paperback on the floor. "I'm selfish. They won't let us work together so I have to take advantage for as long as possible."

"So you think I should take the job?"

"That has to be your decision. I'm not going to influence you. I have an agenda. I want you in this country where you can tie me to the bed, not down some hole in the ground somewhere on the other side of the planet. Mines are dangerous."

"And spying for the security services isn't?"

"Not in the same way. You can't mitigate for a rock falling on your head."

"I think you need to stop worrying."

"Make me."

"Oh, it's like that is it?"

Syd batted his lashes. "Got to make the most of you, haven't I?"

"Take your clothes off."

"What?"

"You heard me. Don't make me tell you again."

"But we're outside…"

"Syd, there's no one here but us. The garden isn't overlooked and it's a beautiful day so unless you're concerned about the sheep on the fells getting their binoculars out for a look, strip. Now."

"I'm more concerned about a bee stinging my dick. Imagine how big and swollen it would get!"

There was an area of lawn in front of their loungers, surrounded by rose beds. The flowers were in full bloom, their fragrance heady and intoxicating. A cool breeze helped with the heat and for once, the humidity of a British summer wasn't too extreme. There was a picnic rug slung over the back of his seat so Oberon spread it on the grass.

"Wouldn't want your bits tickled."

"Funny. Check for thistles in that grass." Syd stepped out of his shorts. He wasn't wearing underwear and was already hard.

"The only thing that's going to be pricking your sensitive behind is me," Oberon said.

"Got any lube?"

"As it happens, I do."

"You were planning this!"

"No need for the fake outrage, brat. On your knees."

"Love it when you get bossy."

"I know." Oberon smirked. His cock jerked as Syd dropped to his knees, thighs spread wide, resting his backside on his heels. "Fuck, you're beautiful." Oberon admired Syd's sun-kissed skin, noting the faint tan lines and familiar freckles. Even after a recent cut, his hair was a tousled mess and there was a dusting of stubble on his chin. "Edible."

"Hey! I am *not* a snack."

"Debatable." Oberon took his time removing his clothes, giving Syd a show. The way he was licking his lips suggested Syd appreciated the effort. "Like what you see?"

"Yum. The scars are sexy. Though I'd rather you avoided getting any more."

Oberon traced the line on his shoulder. The surgeons had done a good job. He avoided thinking about the blood loss and how close he'd been to never seeing Syd again. He focused instead on his kneeling boyfriend.

"Less talking, more sucking." He stood in front of Syd, fisting his erection.

"Mine."

Oberon pushed at Syd's lips. "Open wide." Syd seemed intent on bringing Oberon to a rapid orgasm, sucking like his dick was an ice lolly in a heatwave. Oberon grabbed his hair, forcing him to slow down. "You're too good at this."

Syd made an incoherent response and kept going until Oberon stepped back. Syd pouted. "I was enjoying that."

"You want me filling your ass or not?"

"What kind of a stupid question is that?" Syd got onto his hands and knees. He wiggled his butt.

Oberon knelt behind him. "We've both had test results back now…do you want, I mean I can still glove up if you'd prefer."

"No! I mean, yes! No condoms ever again."

"Have you ever gone bare before?" Oberon asked.

"No. You?"

"No."

"Uh, Obi, much as I appreciate the significant nature of this moment, do you think we could appreciate it *after* you're done fucking the life out of me? Pretty please." Syd glanced over his shoulder.

Oberon shook his head. He slathered lube over his cock then gave Syd's backside a messy slap. "You need prep?"

"It's been all of six hours…I think I can cope."

Oberon smacked him again. "That's for being cheeky when I'm being considerate.

"Ow!"

Despite Syd's assurances, Oberon pushed a lubed finger into his channel. "Hot and tight. Perfect."

"Seriously? This is not some cheap porn flick. Stop teasing and get in me!"

"Always so impatient." Oberon relented and replaced his finger with his dick. "Fuck, you feel good." The heat made him languorous and relaxed. He rested a hand on Syd's hip and pushed deep inside him. The absence of a barrier between them seemed to sensitize his shaft. Each thrust brought new sensations.

Syd moaned and urged him to move faster. "Need to come, Obi...harder!"

"On your side." Oberon pulled Syd down with him, still joined. He curled around him and slung an arm over his hip, reaching for his cock.

"Oh God!" Syd wrapped his hand over Oberon's, making him squeeze tighter. Oberon jacked Syd's shaft in time with his thrusts. A bird, chasing a damsel fly, swooped over them and Syd gasped his release. He froze, caught in the moment as his muscles corded with effort, then relaxed with a contented sigh. Oberon withdrew almost completely then sank deep into Syd's channel with one forceful push. He came, jubilant that his cum now painted Syd's channel. He held him close, not wanting to lose the moment.

"That was perfect," Syd murmured.

"More different than I expected," Oberon said. "Better."

"*So* much better, and we did it pretty good already."

"No harm in practicing though."

They finally drew apart and lay side by side on the blanket, staring at the sky. "That cloud looks like a sausage dog," Syd observed.

Oberon stared at it. "It does."

Syd entwined his fingers with Obi's. "I didn't tell you, Fran rang last night. She met Ed for a drink. They hit it off right away."

"We should warn him. He doesn't stand a chance."

"Knowing Fran it's already too late and besides, won't Ed adore the idea of being a writer in a castle?"

Oberon chuckled. "Yeah. I can see him fitting right in. We'll have to go visit."

"You have to meet my parents. Wow, this *is* getting serious."

"I hope so." Oberon squeezed Syd's hand. "We have something really good here, don't we? I am planning on taking that job. It feels like there's still a lot to do tracking down the remnants of Black Stone, making sure Kairos Doukas doesn't fake die again…"

"Yay!" Syd tumbled on top of him, peppering his face with kisses. "That's amazing. You can move in with me in London and…"

"Wait, what? You want me to move in with you?" Oberon cupped Syd's face. "Are you sure?"

"Of course. I love you, you big dummy." Syd blushed to the roots of his hair. "Oops. That slipped out."

Oberon shifted his hands to Syd's bottom then rolled him over so that Syd was flat on his back. "I guess it's good I love you too then."

"Yeah?" Syd's lower lip quivered.

"Don't you dare cry on me."

"The sun's in my eyes," Syd said, scrubbing at them. "Not crying."

Oberon kissed away the salty trails on Syd's cheeks. "Lie like that again and I'll introduce your ass to my snappiest crop." He cut off Syd's reply with a long, deep kiss. The sun played across Oberon's back and the heady scent of flowers filled the air. Things wouldn't always be so serene and that was okay. Syd would keep life interesting.

"More kisses!" Syd demanded.

"Bossy brat..." Oberon let Syd pull him close. Their lips touched and in that moment, nothing else mattered.

Sign up for our newsletter and find out about all our romance book releases, eBook sales and promotions, sneak peeks and FREE romance books!

Want to see more from this author?
Here's a taster for you to enjoy!

The Augur: Seeing Death
L.M. Somerton

Excerpt

"Your parents would have been very proud of the young man you've become, Bryn. You're going to love college."

Bryn Ashton cupped his mug of hot chocolate and eyed his housemother warily. "I sense a but coming on."

"Buuuut…can you please curb that sharp tongue of yours. Make some friends. Be nice."

"I knew the marshmallows on the top of this were a bribe."

"Bryn…"

"I know! I only get one chance and I won't mess up, promise. That's if I don't turn into some monster freak tomorrow. There used to be a time when people looked forward to their eighteenth birthdays, right?"

Annie Cormac shook her head. "In the thirty years I've been running group homes, I've not had a single kid turn into a monster. A couple werewolves and one vamp. That's it. All three of them have gone on to successful careers and happy lives. They are *not* monsters. No one affected by the gene mutation is, and I won't have you using that word in this house."

"Sorry, Annie."

"I should think so. I know the virus killing your parents has been hard but remember, they were part of the team that found the cure."

"I don't remember them, you know that. I was a baby when they died, and no different from thousands of other kids whose parents were taken. I'm not complaining."

"Fifty years to find a cure. So many deaths."

"And so many people with traits we all thought were the stuff of movies and books. What if I..."

"None of that now. Even if you do turn out to be lupine or sanguine, it'll make little difference. You'll have to take an additional minor at college is all, so that you learn to cope with the changes to your body. A good portion of men in the military, police force and fire service are wolves now. Vamps make great doctors and scientists."

"But what if I'm...different?"

"Oh, honey, other changes are so rare that's very unlikely. You'll wake up tomorrow and be your usual grumpy self."

"I can't imagine how much of a crap fest it would be to discover you can suddenly read minds or predict the future like some kind of oracle."

"Which is why people like that have to be protected by the authorities. How many seers or augurs have you heard of in your lifetime? I can only recall one, so stop worrying. You've got more chance of winning the lottery."

"I guess. How does the gene even know when a person reaches eighteen? Is it in there putting crosses on a calendar or something—like its counting down to Christmas?"

"That's one of several mysteries yet to be solved. Same as why the virus was only fatal to certain age groups while others didn't even know they had it, and why the virus only activates the gene in males."

"There'll be lots of kids like me at college, won't there?"

"Sure will. Fifty percent of kids in your generation grew up in group homes just like this one."

Bryn drained his mug. "I want tomorrow to be over so I can get back to worrying about my college roommate turning out to be a trombone player. Normal stuff." He shoved his chair back. "Thanks for the chocolate, Annie. I'll be in my room embracing my Goth tendencies."

"Keep the volume down." Annie pulled him into a hug. "What will be, will be, Bryn. Try to get some sleep."

Bryn left the familiar warmth of the kitchen and climbed three flights of stairs to his attic room. As the current oldest ward of the group home, he had a room to himself. Everyone else had to share, which he'd also had to do until the previous eldest had moved out two years before. In a house full of noisy kids ranging in age from four to seventeen, his room was his sanctuary. It was a quiet place to study and to dream. He couldn't wait to leave for college and the government funded full-ride scholarship that would allow him to study biochemistry. One day he wanted to join the team researching the effects of the virus that had taken his parents. The cure was a recent discovery and though future generations might be protected by infant vaccination, it didn't work on those who had already turned.

It was getting late and he should sleep. Tomorrow there would be a cake and gifts, even though for him the celebration would be tinged with sadness. Reaching eighteen meant that his time at the group home was coming to an end. It was all he'd ever known but he had his college place and in two weeks would be moving on. He had to pack up his life into a few boxes and leave Annie and the other kids behind. It was exciting and terrifying at the same time.

His room was a reflection of his personality. The walls were covered with posters of indie rock bands begged from the downtown record store. His shelves were stacked with an eclectic mix of books on topics as diverse as archeology to zoology and fiction covering everything from horror and thrillers to the classics. Reading had always been an escape and Bryn's part-time job bagging groceries at the neighborhood store had funded his addiction.

He picked up a framed photo of his parents. The smiling people staring back at him were strangers but he had inherited his mother's black hair and his father's green eyes and pale skin. The mixture of Irish and Hispanic heritage from generations back had come through strong in him. He'd been a late child, a welcome surprise after years of trying, and because of that his grandparents had all passed on. Neither of his parents had any siblings, which meant that when the virus took them he was left alone. If he had any relatives anywhere, he didn't know about them and presumably they had no idea he existed. No one had ever tried to claim him.

Kicking off his battered boots, Bryn stretched out on his bed. He didn't undress because he had yet to make a pre-sleep trip to the bathroom, which was on the floor below. He had on black jeans and a black T-shirt — there were no other colors in his wardrobe. He spotted a hole in one sock and wiggled a pale toe. *Maybe vamping out wouldn't be too bad.* He tongued an incisor. *It's not like sanguines turn into bats or anything, just need more red meat than most and high factor sunscreen. Don't think I'd make a great wolf though, they're way too energetic.* Those with the wolf gene were stronger, faster and usually hairier than an average human. They did not howl at the moon, silver didn't kill them and they didn't turn into slavering beasts. No painful bone cracking or shredding of clothes. *All the myths and legends are a crock of shit but they have to mean that the genes have been active in the past. They must have been dormant and the virus reactivated them somehow.* That was the working theory anyhow. Meanwhile, boys reaching maturity continued to approach their birthdays with trepidation.

"Annie's right, of course. Fuck all I can do about it," Bryn grumbled. He cracked a yawn and took that as a signal to head for the bathroom. Morning would come soon enough and he wanted to face it with a clear head.

"Nightmares suck." A few short hours later, Bryn lay in bed staring at the ceiling. A crack in the plaster travelled the full width of the room. Bryn had named it San Andreas and had watched its progress over the last two years with morbid curiosity, wondering if he'd wake one morning covered in plaster and looking at the sky. Light filtered through the institutional gray blinds, telling him his birthday had arrived. *Hmm, don't feel any different.* He raised one arm. Not any hairier. A peek beneath the covers showed him a chest still bereft of a single, solitary hair. "Not a wolf then." He prodded his teeth. They didn't seem any pointier than usual and he wasn't craving raw steak for breakfast. "Not a vamp either. Wow. Totally normal." Pushing away the remnants of his bad dream from his mind, he swung his legs out of bed. He sat for a moment, shrugged then went through his usual morning routine before dressing and heading for the kitchen.

The moment he walked in, ten eager faces turned his way. Expressions ranged from boredom to curiosity to outright fascination. Bryn held up a hand. "Before any of you brats say a word, no, not a wolf, not a vamp. Just me."

He was swarmed by a crowd of kids who all apparently needed to check him over in person. Summoning his last ounce of patience, he stood still for an entire minute before shedding them. The youngest he tucked under one arm before depositing her on a chair where she dissolved in giggles.

"Annie, please tell me there's coffee."

"Do I look like your maid? It's in the pot. Pancakes are on the way."

Bryn dragged himself to the coffee pot, poured a mug, downed it then got himself a refill before he resumed his seat. He was no longer the center of attention and conversations carried on around him. He poured juice for the little ones then broke up a fight over the cereal boxes. His head pounded.

"Didn't sleep well, huh?" Annie deposited a plate of fluffy pancakes in front of him. "Birthday boy gets the first stack."

"Thanks, Annie and no, I didn't. Weird dreams."

The familiar chaos of breakfast carried on around Bryn and he let it wash over him. The other kids were great but his tolerance was limited, particularly first thing in the morning. Annie slid two Tylenol his way.

"Lifesaver." He swallowed the tablets with more coffee.

"You should switch to decaf and I can't believe I need to say that to an eighteen year old." Annie waved a batter-coated spatula at him.

"Noted."

Next came gifts. There were pictures and crafts from the littlies and the three biggest had pooled a few dollars to get him a black ceramic take-out cup with a skull and cross bones on it. "I love it." Bryn was genuinely touched. "It'll be so useful at school. Thanks, guys."

Annie gave him a hand-knitted black scarf with a single pale blue line across each end. "It'll get cold at Harvard." She hugged him and suddenly he was mobbed with lots of warm bodies, all demanding hugs. Tears pricked at his eyes.

"You guys! Stop!" The kids drifted away and Bryn was left with Annie. "That was…sweet."

"They like you, despite that emo façade you put on."

"Hey!"

"We'll have cake after dinner tonight, okay?"

"Yeah. I'm full of pancakes now."

"I've put a little money in the bank account we set up for you…no arguing, it's what you're due. A little kick-starter for college books, that kind of thing."

"I don't know what to say. Thank you."

"That'll do. How's the head?"

"Pounding. Strange—I don't tend to get headaches." Bryn knuckled his temples. "Think I'll go lie down. Try to catch up on some of the sleep I didn't get last night. Now I know I'm not…special."

"You'll always be special to me, sweet cheeks." Annie ruffled his hair.

Bryn made gagging noises. "Stop already!"

"Go to bed."

The next thing Bryn knew was someone shaking him awake. He groaned and cranked an eyelid. "Annie?"

"Hey, Sleeping Beauty. You've been out cold for eight hours. You need to get your rear downstairs."

Annie yanked open the drapes, flooding the room with light. "I hope you haven't picked up the flu or something."

"Ow, fuck!" Bryn hid beneath the covers. Sleep had not improved his headache.

"Language, young man. The screening bureau officer is downstairs eating my cookies. You need to come show him the gene hasn't activated."

"Sorry. Okay. On it. Give me two seconds." He winced at the door closing, the noise pounding his skull like a jackhammer. He grabbed his shades and put them on. Gently. Shielding his eyes from the light helped a bit. *Must have been more stressed out about today than I realized. This has to be a migraine.*

Bryn counted it a win that he made it down the stairs without falling on his ass. Annie was waiting with the official in the TV room. They were both seated on the sectional, chattering away like old pals.

"Here he is, Charlie. The latest of a long line."

"And no indications?"

"None. He's his normal teenage self."

"Oh dear. Congratulations on your birthday, Bryn. I'm Charles Donovan from the screening bureau and this visit is nothing to worry about." He held out a hand and Bryn shook it.

"Hey."

"I'm going to give you a finger prick for a blood sample. It's a quick and easy test for gene activation which shows us sanguine or lupine indications. A visual assessment isn't always accurate."

Bryn slumped on the sectional trying not to look as belligerent as he felt. "This is pointless."

"Probably," Charlie said. "But wouldn't you rather have it noted on your record that you have no active gene so that you don't have people hounding you in the future?"

"I suppose."

"Be nice, Bryn." Annie's warning tone was enough to have him sitting a bit straighter.

Charlie got out his testing kit. "Don't worry, you won't miss the tiny bit I'm going to take." He jabbed Bryn's middle finger pad then collected a bead of blood on a dropper that went into a tiny test tube of clear liquid. "It's red at least."

"You say that to everyone, don't you?" Bryn muttered.

"Sure do. Perk of the job. Right, I'm looking for what color the liquid changes to. Lupine goes green, sanguine is purple. No gene change is golden yellow." He shook the tube.

"So what the fuck is sky blue?" Bryn felt sick. He stared at the little glass vial.

"I…need to make a call. Don't move." Charlie went into the hall.

Bryn watched him go. "Annie, what's happening?"

"I don't know." She came to sit next to him on the couch and grabbed his hand.

A pulse of sharp pain shot through Bryn's already throbbing head and his vision dimmed. In his head he had a picture of Annie standing in the dock of a courtroom facing a judge. She looked resigned. Bryn yanked his hand away in horror and the image faded.

"If you go now, you'll have time to grab a few things and get out through the back yard," Annie whispered. "I'll tell Charlie you went to the bathroom."

"What? Why would I do that?"

"Because if that test is showing that you have some rare variation of the gene, you'll be taken by the security services and put through God knows what kind of experimentation while they work out what you can do."

"And if I run, they'll hunt me down. When you touched me Annie, I saw…well, let's just say things wouldn't work out well for you either." It was tempting to try it. Bryn thought he could make a good go of disappearing, but he couldn't do that to Annie. If she was blamed, what would happen to all the other kids in her care? He wasn't that much of an asshole.

"You shouldn't think about me. I'd happily go to court for you. Be selfish. Go."

Bryn slumped on the couch. "No. Not an option." Tentatively, he touched Annie's hand. He flinched at the pain but now the image in his head was of a smiling Annie watching over kids playing in the yard. His vision cleared and he sighed. "I guess Harvard is off the cards. Fuck."

When Charlie came back into the room he seemed tense. "Your test result is…unusual, Bryn. You felt fine this morning?"

"Yeah, apart from a headache. I didn't sleep well last night. It got worse though."

"Do you know what time you were born?"

"Eight-thirty in the morning," Annie contributed. "It's in his records."

"Gene activation can be very precise. The change must have happened after you got up this morning. Would you take off your sunglasses for me?"

Hand trembling, Bryn removed the glasses. The light hurt his eyes.

"Oh my." Annie stared at him.

"What?" Panicked, Bryn went to look in the mirror on the mantel over the fire. "Fuck me." His eyes were a far brighter shade of green than they had been and they seemed backlit, glowing like a cat's in the dark. He put the glasses back on. "They weren't like that earlier."

"There'll be a car here for you shortly. More tests will need to be done. I can come with you to your room, if you want to pack a few things."

"When will I be back?" Bryn asked the question even though he already knew the answer.

"Not sure. It could be a while."

He means never. Why me? Bryn wanted to scream but decided it would hurt his head too much. "Fine. You and the kids will have to share that cake, Annie."

Charlie trailed him up the stairs then stood in the doorway while Bryn threw a few things in a duffel.

"You thought about running, didn't you?"

"Maybe."

"What stopped you?"

"Annie's been as close a thing to a mother I've ever had. She doesn't deserve trouble because of me."

"Yeah, she's one of the good ones."

"Has this ever happened to you before… I mean the blue reaction?"

"Never. I've had a few wolves in my time and one or two vamps. This was new."

"Great. Just fucking great." *Should have bought that lottery ticket.*

"You done? Let's go see if the car's here."

Some of the other kids had gathered in the hall. There was a clamor of questions. Annie ushered them away and raised a hand in farewell. "Good luck," she mouthed.

Bryn gave her what he hoped was a reassuring smile rather than a grimace. When the door closed behind him it had an air of finality.

"They're here," Charlie announced.

A black SUV with heavily tinted windows drew up at the curb. Two armed men in black fatigues got out and one walked over. The other stayed by the vehicle, scanning the street as if he expected an attack to come out of nowhere at any moment.

"This him?" The man addressed Charlie.

"What am I, invisible?" Bryn muttered.

"It is. I sent through his test result already." Charlie took a step back.

"He give you any trouble?"

"Seriously? Does it look like I did?" Bryn made a conscious effort not to be intimidated by the excessive amount of firearms the guy carried.

"Get in the fucking car."

"A please wouldn't go amiss." Bryn stomped down the path. He tossed his duffel into the back seat then climbed in after it. He was followed by one of the men in black and before Bryn could come up with a suitable epithet, the guy stuck him with a needle. "What the actual…" He didn't get to finish the sentence before the lights went out.

* * * *

Bryn came around with a start. He wasn't sure what had woken him but had a vague sense that it had been a sharp noise. His headache had faded a bit but he was groggy and confused. "Where the fuck am I?" He was sitting on a plastic chair, head lolling, in a room that was in serious need of interior decoration. The gray walls were less than inviting. There was one door and a large interior window across one wall. He lifted his head, wincing at the crack his neck gave. *Has to be an interrogation room. There are probably people behind that window watching me.* It was then he realized that his wrists were cable tied together. *This just gets better and better.* He raised both hands then gave the window the finger. *Juvenile, I know but it makes me feel better.* There was a table in front of him so he laid his head on his arms and closed his eyes. *They'd better not have lost my shades.*

A few minutes later, the door opened. Footsteps crossed the room and someone occupied the chair on the other side of the table. Bryn's curiosity got the better of him and he raised his head. The man facing him looked to be in his forties, with silver flecked dark hair and gray eyes. Everything about him was non-descript, as if he dressed deliberately to blend into the background. He pinned Bryn with a sharp gaze.

"How are you feeling, Bryn?"

"Like someone drugged me without my permission," Bryn muttered. "Where am I?"

"You were drugged specifically so that you wouldn't know your location. It means you can't tell anyone else and that helps us protect you."

"Protect me from what, exactly?"

"If you turn out to be what we think you are, it makes you valuable. Criminal elements will want to get their hands on you and at the moment, you're defenseless."

"So why are my hands tied? Unless you guys have a bondage fetish?"

"That's to stop you accidentally touching someone. It makes you more aware of where your hands are."

"And you don't want me touching anyone because…"

"We think you may be an augur."

Bryn stared at him. "And what exactly is that?"

"I think you already know that. There have been two examples in the last thirty years of blue tests like the one you had today. Both of those people were able to see the future in some way. One could also look into past memories." The man paused. "Charlie told me that he thought you'd already experienced something like that today. Tell me about that."

"How about you tell me who you are and why I should trust you, because I have to say you're not making the best first impression."

"I work for the government, Bryn. For the organization that monitors and takes care of those who are gene gifted."

"Gifted. Right. You have a name?"

"Call me Warden or Sir, whichever you prefer."

"I wish I hadn't asked."

"The more cooperative you are, Bryn, the easier things will be. Now tell me what happened this morning."

Bryn sighed. He didn't want to spend more time on the uncomfortable chair than was necessary. "My housemother, Annie…after we saw the test this morning, she grabbed my hand. In my mind, I saw her in a courtroom. Then, after I realized that trying to get away is what would put her there, and I decided not to run, I touched her again. The images changed and she was safe and happy."

The warden grunted. "Sounds like you saw her intent. And you haven't had visions about anyone else since?"

Bryn shook his head. "Nope, but your thugs knocked me out, remember?"

"Okay, this is what's going to happen. You'll be taken from here to a training facility. A kind of school, if you like. There, specialists will endeavor to gauge your abilities and test them. Alongside that you will receive a college-level education, a health and fitness program and psychological support."

"And I guess I get no choice in the matter?"

"None. This is a government requirement for somebody like you and is all clearly defined in law."

"And how long am I supposed to stay at this place?"

"Between two and three years, depending on your progress and the strength of your abilities."

"And after that?"

"To be determined. Potentially, a job in the security services."

"What do the other people who tested blue do now?"

"They don't. They didn't survive their training."

On that note, Warden stood and left the room. Bryn stared at the closed door. *Wonderful. I am well and truly fucked.*

About the Author

LM lives in a small village in the English countryside, surrounded by rolling hills, cows and sheep. She started writing to fill time between jobs and is now firmly and unashamedly addicted.

She loves the English weather, especially the rain, and adores a thunderstorm. She loves good food, warm company and a crackling fire. She's fascinated by the psychology of relationships, especially between men, and her stories contain some subtle leanings towards BDSM.

LM is a past winner of the National Leather Association International's Pauline Reage Award for best novel and John Preston award for short fiction. She has twice won the Golden Flogger Award for best BDSM novel in the LGBT category. She has received multiple Honorable Mentions in the Rainbow Awards and won the Action and Adventure category of Divine Magazine's Book Awards.

LM Somerton loves to hear from readers. You can find her contact information, website details and author profile page at https://www.firstforromance.com

ENTWINED PUBLISHING